Count a Hundred Stars

Count a Hundred Stars

Bonnie Wisler

Copyright © 2010 by Bonnie Wisler.

Library of Congress Control Number: 2010902170
ISBN: Hardcover   978-1-4500-4757-9
              Softcover   978-1-4500-4756-2
              Ebook   978-1-4500-4758-6

All rights reserved. No part of this book may be reproduced or transmitted in any form or by any means, electronic or mechanical, including photocopying, recording, or by any information storage and retrieval system, without permission in writing from the copyright owner.

This is a work of fiction. Names, characters, places and incidents either are the product of the author's imagination or are used fictitiously, and any resemblance to any actual persons, living or dead, events, or locales is entirely coincidental.

This book was printed in the United States of America.

To order additional copies of this book, contact:
Xlibris Corporation
1-888-795-4274
www.Xlibris.com
Orders@Xlibris.com
76765

PROLOGUE

"WHERE'S THE MONEY?" he asked, his speech raspy and strained, his appearance foul. Greasy strands of dyed hair lay plastered to his scalp. Short, swollen hands with dirty unclipped nails grasped a plain manila envelope.

Her skin crawled to even sit across from him; but she was willing to do whatever was necessary to find out if her lover was cheating on her. "It's here, in the bag. I don't want everyone in this dive to know I've got a lot of money on me."

She surveyed her surroundings. A jukebox in the corner spun classic rock mixed with honky-tonk, while men dressed in black leather and decorated with multi-colored tattoos drank beer and shot pool in the dimly lit bar. It was one o'clock in the afternoon; didn't these people work?

The creep sitting across from her definitely wasn't her first choice and she didn't like doing business with him, but he was cheap. And from what her friend told her, his morals wouldn't interfere with the job. Good. The first detective she contacted told her she was crazy and refused her business. How dare he? No one would keep her away from Roger. No one.

She knew the detective had set up the meeting in the biker bar to piss her off. He didn't like her and wanted everything his way. That was OK; she didn't like him either. But she showed him. Just for spite, she wore a stylish wrap dress, Gucci sunglasses, and pulled her dark red hair into a French twist.

"Give it to me. Now! I don't have time to play games with an uppity bitch like you," he demanded, and snatched his envelope off the table. He pulled a pack of cigarettes out of his shirt pocket and slid one out, catching it between yellowed teeth.

"Don't get crazy on me. I said I have the money." She fidgeted in her seat and looked around the bar again. A haze of smoke clung to the ceiling. Damn! Her back was to the door. How had that happened? Tricking him into taking only part of the money was out of the question now . . . "I need to see at least one picture before I pay you. Not that I don't trust you," she said in a sweet, southern accent, forcing a smile and half laugh.

He leered across the wooden booth at her and snickered as he tapped the cigarette against the wood. "Is a kiss enough, or do you want a picture of them doing the deed?" His eyebrow arched with the question; his eyes narrowed. Spit clung precariously between his top and bottom lip. "Here you go Miss Priss. Here's your prince charming—feeling up his Maid Marion," he replied, tossing one of the photos across the table.

She couldn't believe her eyes. A cold sweat washed over her. It was a compromising pose of her lover with his hands on the breasts of another woman, in the throes of a passionate kiss. It looked as though it had been taken through a kitchen window. Nothing is sacred, not even the kitchen.

She laughed out loud, acting as though she didn't really care, and tossed the brown bag filled with money across the booth at the sleazy detective.

"This is exactly what I needed. Remember—you've never seen me," she said in a low voice. She grabbed the envelope of pictures and quickly exited the smoky bar. Outside, she could breathe again. She glanced over her shoulder and then hurried to the safety of her car.

The locks clicked on the car doors as she settled in, opened the envelope, and dumped the pile of pictures onto the passenger seat. Her hands trembled. Slowly she picked up a photo of a couple walking hand-in-hand by a lake. Placing her thumb over the face of the woman, she gently traced the outline of the man with her finger.

God, he was gorgeous. She loved him so much. It wasn't his fault—he was just a stupid, vulnerable man.

Lifting her thumb she glared at the woman in the photo. The blonde bitch—it was all her fault; she was trying to confuse him and make him feel guilty. She had her chance and blew it. Well it wouldn't work—no games this time.

She held the picture up like a sacrificial offering and slowly began to rip it in half, careful to tear it down the middle of the woman's face.

"This one's for me, Mama. This one's for me," she whispered in homage to her own mother's act of vengeance. She smiled then, as her thoughts drifted to getting the blonde out of the picture for good.

CHAPTER 1

HOPE HANSON FELT like a fish out of water riding down the escalator into the commuter flight area at the Salt Lake City airport. Jeans, boots, and cowboy hats were the prevalent attire but she was still dressed for her morning meeting—gray silk suit, pearls, and heels. Her feet ached. She should have at least brought along a change of shoes. She wasn't used to walking miles through airports in heels.

It had turned into a long day—maybe it was because of that mimosa at 9 AM. But she felt obligated to celebrate, anything to get her client to sign the dotted line; she needed that sale to pay her rent and get her finances back on track. Lately, real estate closings had been few and far between. She could blame half of her money problems on the economy. The other half was *definitely* her fault.

A seat in the corner of the gate area looked like a good place to rest her weary feet. She slipped off her shoes and wiggled her toes. It felt so good to take off those heels.

An old man with a weathered face and brilliant green eyes partly shaded by a cowboy hat found a seat across from her. His eyes were piercing and his face colored from fresh sun. He must have been a real heart breaker in his day . . . maybe he still was.

Her gaze wandered around the gate area. A young couple across the way fussed over crying twins, trying everything they knew to quiet the pair. Dare she hope they wouldn't be on her flight? Sitting by the gate agent's podium was an older lady wearing a mid-calf, cotton print dress and holding tight to her handbag. Off to the side, a tall cowboy with pointed boots hugged a pay phone.

This was definitely not the South.

The gate agent announced the flight and passengers gathered, following single-file through a secured door to the ramp area. Dark gray clouds clutched at the surrounding mountains, providing a beautifully eerie sight. The smell of rain permeated the air.

Hope crossed the tarmac and climbed the steps of the small aircraft. Inside, she stored her briefcase and carryon in the overhead bin and tightly fastened her seatbelt. Her gaze remained on the storm clouds; they looked ominous, like wrinkled, gray fingers lacing around the neck of the mountains. It would be a rough flight.

This was the worst part of the trip. Flying in small planes was not her most favorite form of travel, but it beat walking. Hopefully, once they got up over the clouds, the flight wouldn't be too rough.

Airline personnel scurried around, loading bags and preparing for takeoff. Just as they were ready to close the door, the tall cowboy dashed across the tarmac and bounded up the stairs, two at a time.

"Whew. Just made it!" he announced, stooping as he entered the plane so as not to hit his head on the low ceiling. He removed his hat and tossed it into the overhead bin, revealing dark curly hair. "This must be my lucky day," he quipped, and winked at Hope as he found his seat across from her and tried to get comfortable. His long legs resisted the confinement of the small commuter plane.

She watched while he wiggled around, finally settling in.

"You're going to sit like that for an hour?" she asked, amazed at how he had forced his body into a pretzel like position in the seat.

A broad smile lit up his face when he looked up. "Believe it or not, there is a method to this . . . I take this flight quite often. As with so much in life, position is everything!" Laugh lines highlighted dark eyes that twinkled with mischief. He pushed a pillow between his head and the aircraft window and closed his eyes. "Good night ma'am . . . just hit me if I snore," he said, grinning like he needed a goodnight kiss.

Well—he sure is full of himself, Hope thought, watching out the window as the small plane lifted off to the west. Her eyes shifted back on the cowboy trying to sleep. He was cute, but he wasn't her type. Years ago she vowed to avoid two types of men—cops and cowboys. Her luck with both had been lousy.

She shook her head to clear her thoughts. What was she doing even thinking about men? No. She was coming out here for a reason and it surely didn't involve men. She desperately needed to clear her head, get some rest, and figure out how to get her life back in order. Maybe her luck was changing. Winning an expense paid trip to a dude ranch in the middle of the Big Horn Mountains sounded like the answer to her prayers, and she wasn't about to blow it by wasting precious time thinking about men.

The hum of the propellers overpowered any desire for further conversation. She put her head back, closed her eyes, and soon drifted off to sleep.

Her body jerked like she had fallen out of bed. Terrifying screams filled the small aircraft. It felt like a nightmare but she knew she was now awake. Her stomach tensed as fear grabbed hold of her and sent a deep shiver through her body. All around, lightning flashed and the aircraft vibrated as it pitched back and forth through the violent storm. It bounced and rocked across the sky as though the black clouds were using it for a mean game of pinball. Her fingers dug into the old plastic armrest, gripping it with all her might. She looked frantically around the airplane for someone to contradict her growing fear.

The weathered old man sat rigid, the look of terror mirrored in his eyes as he too glanced around the small plane. The grandmother in the cotton print dress blessed herself repeatedly and prayed the rosary. The twins were screaming at the top of their lungs.

The cowboy sitting in the seat across the aisle reached over and patted her hand with his large calloused one. "Don't worry pretty lady, it'll be all right. Trust me," he said in a relaxed voice, his coal black eyes were calm. His look conveyed a feeling of protection and his touch was gentle and reassuring, but feeling the weight of his hand on hers was startling. She quickly pulled away and began fidgeting in her seat, straightening her skirt, then once again sought out the security of the armrest.

Under normal circumstances she would have said something about the pretty lady comment, but she didn't think he was trying to impress her—he was probably afraid that she was going to start screaming that the plane was going to crash and they were all going to die. Well, it had crossed her mind.

"These storms pop up along the mountains all the time. The pilots are used to them and we wouldn't have taken off if he didn't think he could handle it." A faint scar on the left side of his cheek disappeared into a dimple when he spoke.

"I hate small planes for this very reason. A large jet can fly through this and you'd never know it," her voice was shaky as she continued, "These little things are like wind-up toys."

He patted her hand again.

"Thanks. I'll be fine now," she said and again pulled her hand away. He was starting to annoy her.

"Scared me a bit too, but we should fly out of it soon," he said. He ignored the fact that she had twice pulled away from him and continued to chat. "You're mighty dressed up tonight. Been to a wedding?"

Oh geez, she thought, now we have twenty questions. She really wasn't in the mood for this; but, he was keeping her mind off the storm, so she should at least be polite.

"No. No wedding," she replied. "I had a business meeting earlier in the day. Actually, I'm on my way to vacation . . . at a dude ranch."

"Which one?" he asked.

"Snowy Creek. I'm really looking forward to getting away from it all for a couple of weeks," Hope replied, thinking back on the wild nights she and her friends spent at the bars and nightclubs in Charlotte. They had adopted *Looking for Love in all the Wrong Places* as their theme song. It had been her only escape after Brian's sudden death, but over the past year it had become a habit she was having a hard time breaking.

"I've had my fair share of city life," the cowboy said shaking his head, "city life and city women—now there's a dead-end road. No, give me Wyoming any day. Out here people say what they mean and mean what they say. Life can be hard, but it's real and doesn't lie to you. You always know where you stand, with the land and the people."

"Let me ask you something, with all the space and long winters, don't you get bored out here?" she questioned, remembering the vastness of the landscapes shown in the brochure.

"If you get bored here . . . well then, you really don't belong. It's kind of like love. Either you're in love or not. In between doesn't work," he stated.

And that's exactly the way love happens, Hope thought, remembering when she left nursing in Atlanta to move to Charlotte with Brian. His smile had charmed her the first time she met him in the ER, and his persistent visits had claimed her heart.

She was still angry about Brian's death. He had been working undercover and never told her. How could he be so selfish? His death devastated her—she felt violated, her emotions raw. Late nights and wine helped her develop a state of numbness—which she knew was leading to her dead end. Her brother had tried to warn her, but she had been in too much pain to listen—until now. It was time to grow up or shut up.

"It seems like we're flying out of the storm," Hope commented, noticing that the plane had leveled out. Clouds and rain continued to block her view from the windows.

"Like I said, these guys know what they're doing. They fly this terrain all the time." He smiled at her and leaned back in his seat.

She turned away from him and watched out the window, hoping that he'd just leave her alone. Maybe if she kept her back to him and face toward the window he'd get the hint.

The sound of landing gear locking into place brought a sense of relief to Hope. Realizing they would soon be safely on ground, she felt a bit like a jerk for the way she reacted to the cowboy's attempt to calm her fears. He may have been annoying, but he meant well.

"I feel like I've been rescued by the good guy in the white hat. Whom should I thank for calming my fears?" she asked.

"Calder Elliott's my name. My hat's not white, but it was my pleasure." His voice was husky and smooth and matched the intensity of his eyes. He really was quite charming; too bad he was a cowboy.

"Enjoy your time at Snowy Creek," he said politely.

"I just hope I don't get bored. Two weeks in the middle of nowhere . . . I'm not use to that much nature!" she laughed, but for a moment, she wondered if two weeks at a dude ranch was the answer to her prayers. Was she ready to grow up?

Calder pulled a pen out of his shirt pocket and began writing on the back of a business card. "Here." He handed her the card. "If you get bored while you're here, give me a call. But I'm betting you don't."

"Then why'd you give me your number?" Hope asked. Even though his coal black eyes, dark curly hair and sexy grin were intriguing, she knew she'd never call. He was a pest enough on the plane, no need to open that door any further.

He sat back in his seat and eyed her, causing her to wonder why he was playing games.

"You said city life and city women were a dead-end. Well I'm a city-woman," she said, thinking that would turn him off.

"Actually, I'm using reverse psychology to face my fears, isn't that what the shrinks tell you to do? You won't call, so basically, you're safe." Calder winked, then added, "But . . . if you should, how would I know it's you?"

For a moment she was puzzled by his question. "Oh. My name is Hope. Hope Hanson," she finally replied, and reached across the aisle to shake his hand. "You know," she teased, "it's a good thing I'm not planning on calling you, because you'd only disappoint me. Somehow I don't see you as the type to sit and wait for the phone to ring."

His eyebrows raised and dark eyes twinkled. "I guess there's only one way to find out . . ."

CHAPTER 2

HIGH WINDS AND heavy rains continued to assault the foothills surrounding the Big Horn Mountains, shutting down the Sheridan airport and forcing the flight to divert to Casper. The airline arranged van service to shuttle the passengers back to Sheridan. It was turning into a marathon day, and Hope was exhausted. "What's another hour or two?" she mumbled as the driver helped her step into the minivan taxi. Thank God the young couple with the screaming twosome decided to stay with family in Casper.

She propped her bag in the corner of the back seat, and leaned against it as a pillow. Maybe now she could continue the nap she'd been trying to take since Salt Lake.

"Mind if I join you?" Calder asked, climbing in and sitting next to her before she could object. He sat close, as though he expected someone else to sit next to him. No one did. He put his hat in the empty space.

He was annoying her again.

The van driver shut the door and slowly pulled away from the airport as twilight approached. Casper seemed quaint and quiet, like a place that hadn't seen a lot of change over the past fifty years. Hope wondered what it would be like to live in such a constant environment. Would it provide a sense of security, or a sense of boredom? And why was she focusing so much lately on being bored? If she had nothing to keep her busy would she find out she didn't like herself? Then what?

As they began heading out of town onto the open road, she leaned her head back and closed her eyes; they rode for some time in silence.

Calder's leg brushed against her as the van turned a corner, and the image of his hand on hers flashed through her mind, prompting unexpected thoughts. What was it about this guy? Maybe it was because he had been honest about not being interested in city women and she felt a bit guilty for the way she had treated him. Or maybe it was the way he had teased her about calling. But whatever the reason, thoughts of the long-legged cowboy, with eyes as dark as his hair, taunted her senses. Imagined visions of those strong hands on soft skin shocked her, but also brought a faint smile to her lips.

"You'll like Sarah and Sam," Calder quietly announced, "they're the owners out at Snowy Creek. They really take great pride in their ranch, and have a good variety of activities to keep you busy. Do you ride?"

"Mm-hmm. My brother, Cliff, has a small farm south of Atlanta. He trains and boards horses, and I always ride when I visit. I understand Snowy Creek has some fine horses and one of the best riding programs around—for all levels. I'd hate to have to spend weeks riding around a ring, I want to roam the countryside."

"You'll do that and more. They have a beautiful spread. It backs up to the Big Horn National Forest. During the year, Sam and I pack into the mountains for some fly-fishing—weather permitting. Storms can come up quick in the mountains." He continued on, describing their fishing trips, the snow-capped mountains, crystal clear streams, and the reverent sound of falling snow.

"Sounds heavenly," Hope commented. Yes, the ranch sounded wonderful, but what she found almost mesmerizing was Calder's voice. It was deep but not loud—very soothing, and when he described something it was as if she was there with him seeing it at the same time.

"Sarah is noted for her food. She's an excellent chef, and the staff follow her family recipes. Morning, noon, and night you're in for a treat. She has a knack for turning everyday items into gourmet meals."

"Uh-oh, if the food's that good I may have a problem. I'll have to watch it or I won't be able to fit into my jeans," she said, remembering the six weeks of serious dieting to get back into her favorite jeans.

"I hope you don't mind me saying this, but I don't think you have to worry about how you look in your jeans. With legs like yours, I can't imagine you looking anything but fine. As a matter of fact," the twinkle in his eye was back, but the faint scar on his cheek was hidden in the evening shadow, "you'll have all the cowhands at your beck and call. I'll bet Sarah has to give them a talking to so you can have some peace and quiet!"

"I think you'd better quit while you're ahead. I was almost believing you!" Hope chided. Their eyes met in the shadows of the back seat. His dark smiling eyes washed her in warmth, enticing her closer. His leg still lightly pressed against hers and she tightened her thigh, certain that he too realized the contact.

He was a tempting invitation. What it would be like to kiss him, to touch his rough calloused hands and feel them on her skin?

No. Stop. What was she doing, flirting with a cowboy thousands of miles from home? Cowboys and cops—both off limits—remember? She knew better. She couldn't stand sitting across the aisle from him on the plane, why did he suddenly intrigue her? So what was it about him that both calmed and excited her at the same time? Maybe it was the fact that they were strangers, and that she'd never see him again. Or maybe she was just very tired.

"One thing I must warn you about," Calder leaned closer and whispered in her ear, his breath tickled her neck. "The nights in Wyoming are mesmerizing. Under the big sky there are millions of stars, all calling out to you. Legend has it, if you count a hundred stars, your wish will come true!"

"Whose legend?"

"Locals. It's a story that's been passed on from generation to generation," he replied. His dimple got deeper each time he smiled.

"Well . . . . are you going to keep me in suspense or tell me about the legend? I think we have a long ride ahead of us." She settled back in her seat and decided to give him her full attention. After all, it was a long ride.

"It all started with a trapper, and a bitter winter. There came up a deadly blizzard, a white out, and the trapper and his horse were stranded, unable to move through the tremendous drifts. Wind and cold pounded the weary trapper and his horse, but somehow, he found a small space carved out of the side of the mountain, a small cave, and he and his horse sought shelter there. Day turned into night and back into day; the bright white continued. Water was scarce, and food was no more—when suddenly, the blizzard stopped." Calder paused, for effect.

"Go on," Hope urged, charmed with his storytelling talent.

"The night sky cleared, and snow blanketed all the earth. The trapper knew he and his horse would surely die there. They were snowed in and couldn't get out of their makeshift shelter. It was bitter cold. They were trapped. That night the trapper prayed to the Snow God, asking him to take back some of the snow. Just a little. Just enough so they could make their way out of the shelter and down the mountain to the town below to where his true love lived and waited, and surely prayed for his safe return. And that night, he watched in awe and counted. One by one, huge snowflakes whisked away from his tiny shelter to a place high up in the sky, shining bright to light his way back down the mountain. One by one he counted, until he could count no more. One hundred snow stars lit up the sky the night the trapper and his horse escaped near death and trudged through snow drifts to return home. One hundred stars that were there, for the asking, just waiting to light the way and send him to his true love . . . because even the Gods, most of all the Gods, believe in love. They'll remove obstacles and bring pure happiness to your heart. All you have to do is ask." He stared out the window into the night sky, as if trying to count the stars.

"What a beautiful legend," she said softly, not wanting to break the spell, wondering what it must have been like that snowy night long ago. Life back then was so demanding; people didn't have time to be bored. Maybe she was just born at the wrong time.

"I'll bet you tell all us city-slickers the same tale," she added, but kept her eyes downcast, afraid his gaze would draw her in further.

"You're right, I do. But most of them don't believe me."

"The question is—do you believe it?" Hope asked, wondering if he'd answer.

CHAPTER 3

THE SHERIDAN AIRPORT seemed deserted except for a truck with "Snowy Creek" emblazoned on the cab door. The rain had slowed to a drizzle, creating the appearance of halos around the airport lights.

"I'd offer you a ride but it looks as though they're waiting for you," Calder said, nodding in the direction of the ranch truck. "I meant what I said on the plane, but you don't have to be bored to call. If you'd like some company other than four legged, I'd be happy to oblige." He grinned, put on his hat and quickly stepped outside the van. He held his hand out for Hope. She reached for it and stepped out, into mass confusion. Airport personnel and others awaiting transportation converged on them from inside the terminal.

A black pick-up truck beeped its horn and pulled up close. A girl in tight jeans, t-shirt and a black cowboy hat jumped out of the truck and dashed through the raindrops toward Calder. She had dark hair pulled back into a long shiny braid. Hope felt a twinge of jealousy as she watched them hug. They seemed happy to see each other.

"Ms. Hanson?" a young wrangler with an outstretched hand and a wide grin approached Hope. He looked like he was just out of college, with bright green eyes and blonde hair that fell across his forehead. "I'm Justin, and I work at Snowy Creek. I'm here to take you to the ranch."

Hope smiled wearily and reached out to shake his hand. "Hi. I sure am glad to see you! I've got this bag. My briefcase and suitcase are in the back of the taxi," she said. Turning back, her eyes followed Calder and the girl in tight jeans as they climbed into the black truck. He started the engine and blinked the headlights off and on. He waved and blinked the lights again—then moved out of the lot and into the night. She watched until she could no longer see the taillights and knew it would be a cold day in hell before she called him. Now he was really off limits. Not only was he a cowboy, but a cowboy with a girlfriend. No way she'd ever go that route.

"Ms Hanson . . . ."

She turned and faced the young man again. "I'm sorry, it's been such a long day. You have no idea." She shook her head as if even she could not believe she had left home at 6:30 in the morning, closed a sale at the office, then headed to the airport, got on a plane, connected in Salt Lake, to finally arrive in Wyoming at night. She had no idea what time it was, but traveling all day had worn her out. That had to be the reason she was suddenly attracted to Calder, she's exhausted and not thinking straight. Yes. That had to be it.

"I'll have you there in the blink of an eye. Here's the key to your cabin. Sarah and Sam, they run the ranch, they thought you'd be tired and were afraid they may not be up when you arrived, so they asked me to help you settle in. You can check-in and do the paperwork in the morning. Tomorrow night you'll get together with the others for orientation." The ranch hand had a great attitude and she could tell right away that he enjoyed being charged with picking up guests at the airport. He loaded her bags in the back seat and pulled away from the airport, finally heading toward Buffalo, and Snowy Creek.

Justin turned into a regular tour guide, naming every major building and point of interest along the way. A quick stop at the local all-night grocery offered Hope a chance to pick up a few items for the cabin. A bubble bath and glass of red wine would help knock the kinks out. She may have cut down on the drinking, but she wasn't on the wagon.

The small town of Buffalo quickly disappeared behind them as they turned toward the mountains. Gears struggled and the truck pulled hard as it climbed through the Big Horn Mountains. Squeaky wipers reminded them the rain had all but subsided. The moon was trying to reveal itself from behind clouds that still blanketed the area, creating an eerie scene. It was a lonely winding road, and they hadn't passed another car or truck since leaving the grocery.

"It's really dark up here isn't it?" Hope remarked, feeling a bit foolish but concerned about the road conditions and lack of lights.

"Don't worry—I drive this a lot and know all the twists and turns. It can be intimidating though, especially when it snows. Actually we've just crossed onto some of the Snowy Creek property."

Hope wondered if the storm had made her paranoid. This was the second time today she felt nervous traveling, even though Justin was driving safely and kept his eyes on the snaky road. She was glad they were getting close to the ranch.

"Not to scare you, but right around this next bend is what the locals call Spirit Rock. There have been so many wrecks there they say some nights you can actually see the ghosts of those who died, like they are wondering around, lost."

"Oh great, just what I needed to hear, another legend," Hope replied, "I'm not superstitious but a ghost story on a night like this, is the last thing I need to hear." She continued watching out the window, just in case. Turning the bend, the truck headlights flashed on an object off the side of the road, causing Justin to slam on his brakes.

"What was that?" Hope asked, her heart pumping fast as she turned her head and focused on the area behind them.

"It looked like a car ran off the road." Justin said, and shifted the truck in reverse, carefully maneuvering back. Trees and shrubs concealed a large boulder off the side of the road. They also concealed what was left of a car.

"You stay here Ms. Hanson. I'll go check it out." Justin grabbed a flashlight from the glove compartment and made his way to the crash sight. Hope watched as he flashed his light along the skid marks, then on the wreck. The trunk was open, and clothing was scattered about. He approached on the driver's side, shedding light all over the car. Then he focused it inside.

The flashlight dropped to the ground and rolled away from the car as Justin ran back to the truck. The look on his face said it all.

"Oh my God, Ms. Hanson, she's hurt bad, real bad!"

Hope's hand was on the door handle and her feet touched the ground as Justin approached the truck, his face white with fear.

"I was a nurse, maybe I can help. Call 911. Get an ambulance out here right away!" she barked orders as she raced toward the wrecked car, stopping to pick up the flashlight. Adrenaline coursed through her veins. Shining the light in the car Hope saw a scene not unlike those she had seen enter the trauma unit in Atlanta. The glass windshield had shattered and stuck to the woman's bloody face like a mask—making her features surreal, undistinguishable. A teardrop pearl earring forced through the glass on impact, stuck out perpendicular through the shattered windshield.

Hope placed two fingers to the victim's neck, hoping for a pulse. It was faint, but at least she was alive. The woman was lifeless, jammed between the seat and the steering column—either in shock from the accident or internal injuries. There was no way to know. The airbag was the only thing keeping the steering column from piercing her chest. Blood trickled down the side of her face, matting her blonde hair with the shattered glass.

"You're going to be OK. Hang in there." Hope repeated the words as her hand lightly stroked the woman's shoulder, trying to coax her back to consciousness. The front end of the car looked like an accordion against the boulder. It was impossible for Hope to evaluate her condition; they would need the jaws-of-life to remove her before anything could be done to save her.

Justin appeared from the darkness, unsure if he should approach. "She's alive Justin. She has a chance thanks to you." Hope's words of encouragement were as much for Justin's sake as they were for the poor woman trapped in the car.

"The ambulance is on its way—and the police too!" Justin added, as though he was unsure of what to do while they waited.

"Do you have a blanket in the truck? Let's keep her as warm as we can until the ambulance gets here. And keep talking to her—talk about anything, just keep talking." Hope understood the importance of the victim remaining connected, grounded, hoping to keep her from going further into shock. She often wondered if her fiancé Brian would have survived had someone been there with him, instead of being left alone to die in a dark alley, from an undercover drug deal that went south.

The young cowboy returned with a new sheepskin saddle pad and a plaid wool blanket. They moved with caution placing the items along the woman's side and across the small opening between the seat and windshield where she was pinned. They alternated talking to her, making certain at least one of them was always talking, when the sound of sirens in the distance broke through the quiet of the night.

Flashing lights enveloped the accident site as someone set flares on the road and paramedics rushed to the car. Hope and Justin stood back and watched them quickly check her vital signs and insert an IV. They moved with the precision of professionals. Red and white lights continued to illuminate the sight, bringing it all in full view. The vision of the woman pinned in the car against the boulder, with the trunk popped open was surreal. And now, standing back, taking in the full view, Hope realized just how fortunate the woman was to be alive. She leaned against the front of one of the emergency vehicles, watching rescuers manipulate the jaws-of-life.

The sound of stone crunching under foot caught her attention and she turned. A man approached from the shadows; headlights and emergency flashers cast a yellow-red glow on a familiar tall figure in a cowboy hat.

"What are you doing here?" Hope swayed and stumbled as she stood up from her makeshift seat. The events of the day had left her dizzy, lightheaded, and extremely tired. The cold night air brought chills to her.

"Hey—are you alright? Do I need to get a paramedic over here to look at you?" Calder asked, concerned that Hope was reacting to the after shock of dealing with the stress and trauma of coming upon the accident. His strong arms surrounded her shoulder and waist, providing support.

"No I'm fine; nothing a day or two of sleep won't cure," she replied, running her hand across her hair, smoothing it back into her now disheveled chignon. Her nerves were shot and she was glad to see him. "Mmm. If you hold still and promise not to let go, I bet I can be asleep in seconds." She closed her eyes and relaxed into his arms. The rhythm of his breathing and rise and fall of his chest brought an unfamiliar calm and sense of security. For a moment she forgot that she had sworn him off.

"What *are* you doing here?" she asked, peeking through one open eye. "Are you following me or just always around to come to my rescue?" she teased. This was the second time today he had been there for her. He was making it a bit too easy to look forward to their next encounter.

"I'm investigating the accident. Buffalo Chief of Police at your service ma'am!"

His words hit her like a two-by-four, sending a shiver down her spine and triggering her fight or flight response. She broke away from his protective arms, turned and glared at him. What did he say?

"You have got to be kidding me! Buffalo Chief of Police?" Her voice was filled with indignation. This was turning in to a nightmare. Not only was he a cowboy, he was a cop too. She had to put a lot of distance between them and quick.

"Whoa, wait a minute. What are you attacking me for? I'm the good guy—remember?" Calder surveyed her current condition of disarray. The perfect gray suit of earlier was now smeared with dirt and blood. The color in her cheeks was gone, but her blue eyes had turned dark with anger. Blonde curls fell loose around her face. Even tired and disheveled he liked what he saw. "What's going on here Hope—are you in trouble with the law? If there's something you need to tell me . . . were you involved with the accident?"

"The accident? No—of course not. We discovered it on our way from the airport. Thank God we did or that lady wouldn't have made it through the night. She's already in shock, I'm just hoping we found her in time."

The ambulance swung out onto the road, its siren announcing an urgent descent from the mountains. And from the tone of Calder's voice, it was time for her to leave too.

"If you don't mind, I'm exhausted, and I believe your vehicle is blocking Justin's truck. I'd really appreciate it if you'd move it so we can get going," Hope stated in a calmer voice.

Calder studied her. What had caused her sudden mood swing. One minute she was relaxing in his arms and the next she was attacking him. Was she on the run?

"Can we get out of here—now?" she asked Justin as she walked by him on her way to the Snowy Creek truck.

"Certainly Ms. Hanson—I thought you were . . . never mind." He quickened his pace to reach the truck ahead of her and open the door. The step was high and to maneuver it she had to hike up her skirt, revealing long shapely legs.

Calder emerged from the shadows and approached Justin. "It's been an eventful evening. I'm going to finish up my investigation here and will come out to the ranch tomorrow for a written statement from both you and Ms. Hanson. Please tell her to expect me around noon." Calder's eyes remained on Hope as he spoke to Justin. "Take care of her Justin—she's had a pretty rough day."

"Yes sir. And I'll fill Sam and Sarah in on everything." The young wrangler seemed anxious to regain control and thankful for this added responsibility. He shook hands with Calder and got into the truck.

Other emergency vehicles began departing the scene, making it eerily quiet as Justin pulled out onto the highway. The moon slipped behind a thin cloud as they drove away. Neither spoke until the clicking of the turn signal broke the silence. A "Welcome to Snowy Creek" sign marked the dirt road turn off to the ranch property.

"Calder said to expect him tomorrow at noon. He needs to take a written statement." He kept his eyes on the winding road as he spoke. Run off from the storms was still flowing high in the ditches along the gravel drive, making the curvy road treacherous. Headlights darted from left to right as the truck seemed to ricochet through the woods before entering the valley, and arriving at Snowy Creek Ranch.

As shadows of buildings began to appear, Hope wondered why nothing in her life ever went as planned. This was supposed to be a peaceful and relaxing trip, and so far it was anything but. She strained her eyes to get a glimpse of her new surroundings but with only the truck headlamps to light the area, it was hard to get an idea of the layout of the ranch. It seemed quiet enough—but considering the events of the day, were looks deceiving?

CHAPTER 4

THE LOG CABIN was a welcome respite. Appointed with all the charms of home—fluffy pillows perched on the sofa, scented candles on the mantel, fresh cut flowers on the kitchen table, and a welcome basket of fresh fruit and cheese, it was just what she needed. Justin helped with the bags and lit the fire before saying goodnight. An oversized chair and ottoman beckoned to Hope, offering a perfect view from a picture window of the moon, clouds carelessly parting to weave in and around the crescent shape, casting enchanting shadows across the valley.

A brief hunt through several kitchen drawers and cabinets produced a corkscrew and wine glass. She eyed a green and white checked blanket across the back of the sofa and tossed it on the chair.

"After everything I went through today, I deserve this," Hope said out loud as she sliced the cheese and filled her wine glass. She curled up on the chair and wrapped the blanket over her lap and feet. The fire crackled as it slowly burned, taking the chill off the room and warming Hope. Its hypnotic dance was calming. She raised her glass, and toasted a much-needed vacation. Maybe tomorrow she would have time to think about the mess she had made of her life.

*

The wine bottle was half empty when the sun peeked over the mountains and began filling the room with light. Early morning ranch sounds roused Hope from her makeshift bed in front of the burned out fire. Pulling the blanket over her cold nose, she gazed out across the valley. Situated on the side of a hill, the rustic cabin overlooked a small pond, where this morning a moose and her calf were satisfying their thirst. Bursts of steam produced from their warm breath against the brisk morning air rose from their nostrils. The calf frolicked in the area, drinking from the pond and nibbling tender grasses. Long legs wobbled as he cavorted in the grass, never venturing more than a few feet from mother. Beyond, horses and mules nibbled at mounds of hay in a side corral.

A jagged piece of mountain cut into the pink and blue morning sky. Varying shades of green coursed across the landscape, from a deep forest green in the valley shadows to a light fern color where sunlight hurried to dry the morning dew. The pristine beauty of the mountain sunrise reinforced her belief that coming to the ranch was the right thing to do.

The morning chill permeated the one bedroom cabin. Using her blanket as a wrap, she crossed the room and tossed two more logs on the fire. They cracked and sparked, quickly spreading warmth and the homey scent of a fire throughout the cabin. In the kitchen were all the necessities to start a pot of coffee. With the coffee perking, she gathered her bag with toiletries and headed for a long hot shower. Her favorite gray-silk suit, now covered in bloodstains, fell into a pile on the floor.

The hot water stung as it hit her cold naked body. Water pelted her face as she reached back to release the remains of her chignon and shampooed her hair. It was amazing what a good hot shower could do. Washing away makeup and the reminders of yesterday helped her get in the mood to begin exploring her new environment. No more heels and suits, eyeliner and pearls. She turned off the water and stepped out of the shower to prepare for the day.

A black turtleneck and red-plaid flannel shirt were a must this morning after slipping into a snug pair of jeans. She laced up hiking boots, pulled her long blond curls into a ponytail, and decided to follow her nose. She vaguely remembered Justin saying breakfast was served from seven to nine.

The purity of the morning air and panoramic view surprised her as she stepped onto the cabin porch and took a deep breath. It was a stark contrast to the concrete, noise, and gas fumes of home. She knew that, somehow, nature's clarity would help her to regroup, clear her head, and try to figure out what she wanted out of life. It had worked for her as a child. Riding through the woods had a way of simplifying what had seemed to be monumental problems—like what to wear to the school dance or how to get a certain boy to notice her. Looking back, it seemed so easy then. Hindsight always was. But now, the party scene she and her friends were moving in had become a cycle of dashed relationships—and way too many hangovers and missed opportunities. Definitely a dead-end road she needed to get off.

The dining hall was located in a separate log building, allowing a brisk walk to wake up any hidden hunger pangs. A friendly bloodhound joined her along the way and escorted her to the dining hall. The hound found a sunny spot on the porch, circled, and settled in for one of many morning naps. Hope entered a small foyer containing pictures of the ranch in different stages of development. Some of the photos appeared to be quite old. To the right, the foyer opened into a spacious vaulted dining room. A huge open fireplace in the center of the room was the focal point, providing a view of blazing logs from each table in the room. Justin appeared from behind swinging doors and approached with coffee on a tray.

"Well, I didn't expect to see you out and about this early!" he said, escorting Hope across the dining room to a seat near the fire. "I can fix you pancakes, eggs, oatmeal—whatever your heart desires."

"Aren't you the jack of all trades! Since all I had yesterday was peanuts, I feel like I could eat a horse. Oops—I guess I shouldn't say that out here." She giggled and looked around the dining room. Guests were scattered across the large room that was decorated with a mix of rustic leathers, sturdy wood carved chairs and long wood tables. An enormous buffalo head decorated the long kitchen wall.

"Mmm. A bowl of hot oatmeal with a hint of cinnamon sugar would be perfect. And I'd be more than happy to take that cup of coffee off your hands."

"It's all yours. I'll be back in a minute with your breakfast!" he chirped and headed back toward the swinging doors into the kitchen.

Across the room the front door opened and a tall woman with striking features and cropped salt and pepper hair entered. She smiled and spoke to everyone she encountered, then, approached Justin. He produced another cup of coffee and pointed in Hope's direction. She walked directly to Hope's table.

"Good Morning and welcome," she said, reaching across the table to shake hands. Her voice was lively and her smile wide. "You must be Hope Hanson. I'm Sarah, Sarah Porter. My husband Sam and I are fortunate to call Snowy Creek home all year round." Her gestures were broad; pride reflected in her face.

"From what I've seen so far, I'd say you're a pretty lucky couple. The ranch is even more than I expected. It's absolutely beautiful here." Hope liked Sarah right away, her genuine attitude and graciousness seemed the perfect personality for a hostess of a ranch as grand as Snowy Creek.

"Justin told me of your night. Bless your heart, what a way to start a vacation," she remarked, shaking her head. "I just hope that lady makes it.

When Sam spoke to Calder this morning, he said she was barely holding on."

"Was Calder out here this morning?" Hope asked, surprising herself at the sound of anticipation in her voice.

"No. Sam called to invite him to our party tonight over at the saloon. That's when Calder filled him in on the accident. He also said he'd come by some time this morning to get a statement from you and Justin, and asked Sam to relay that message." Sarah recognized Hope's reaction to Calder's name, and continued. "Calder is our Chief of Police in Buffalo, and we're really lucky to have him. He came back to Wyoming after spending a few years with the FBI in Chicago." Sarah took another sip of her coffee. "He's also a very good friend to Sam and I. He said that you were on his flight last night, something about having to land in Casper?"

"We flew through a really bad storm, and apparently it was too bad to land, so they diverted us to Casper, then taxied us back to Sheridan. What a night!" she said, remembering the feel of Calder's body next to her in the dark taxi. Just the thought of him brought a smile to her face.

"Well, I'm a firm believer that everything happens for a reason. It's a good thing your plane was diverted and you were delayed—there is so little traffic on the mountain road at night that lady could have died out there had it not been for you and Justin."

"He did well. I don't think he'd ever seen an accident like that before, but he turned out to be a real trooper. I told him how important it was to keep talking to her, so he chattered up a storm about the rodeo and how he practices whenever he can—how he's knocked seconds off his time; and on and on. I'll bet when she does recover she'll wonder why she suddenly has all this knowledge about barrel racing!" Hope chuckled remembering his nervous prattle and her own rambling as they struggled to keep her alive.

Justin approached from the kitchen with a tray of steaming hot oatmeal, ripe berries, and a fresh pot of coffee.

"Do you mind if I join you?" Sarah asked, pulling out a chair.

"Please do, I'd love to hear more about the ranch and life in Wyoming. It seems like such an idyllic lifestyle, and quite the opposite of what I deal with everyday."

"Ah," Sarah said knowingly. "I hear that quite often. I can't imagine ever living in the city again. I did once, many years ago. I worked at a law firm in Denver, before Sam swept me off my feet and planted me here." The long wood tables sparkled in the shafts of morning sunlight. "I do hope you enjoy your stay with us. Tonight we'll have our official "Welcome Party" over at the Saloon." Sarah pointed to a two-story log building perched by the creek. "Most of our guests will be arriving throughout the day today."

Hope wanted to find out if Calder had accepted the invitation for tonight, but decided against asking. She did wonder if he would bring the brunette from last night with him.

"Are your guests mostly families?" she asked. Hope adored children and knew it would be fun watching the fearless little ones learn to ride; she also wondered if there would be any other singles staying at the ranch. Socializing with couples was OK to a point, but it often became awkward. Life at the ranch would be a lot easier if there were a few single guests too.

"We usually end up with a pretty good mix, mostly families—babies, teenagers, aunts, uncles, and grandparents too. We get quite a few newlyweds—they love the privacy. And believe it or not we get a fair number of singles. All types from all over the country." A look of reminiscence crossed Sarah's face as she recalled past guests. "That's what I love about opening our ranch up to guests—we meet so many interesting people. And we have a lot of repeat customers that feel like my extended family!"

Their talk continued during breakfast providing Hope information about the activities available to her during her stay—unlimited riding, hiking, fishing, overnight pack trips, campfire parties and square dancing at the saloon. There was even a hike to the legendary Hole in the Wall, past the hideouts of Butch Cassidy and The Sundance Kid. But most of all, her time was her time. She could take advantage of the activities or sleep in.

After breakfast Sarah directed Hope down the road to the ranch office to register. The old cabin was one of the first constructed on the ranch for guests. It was an open room with a fireplace on the far wall.

"There are no phones on the property, other than the phone we have in the office. You can give that out as an emergency number and if you get a call we post your message on the bulletin board of the dining room. So make sure to check it."

"I have a cell phone so I should be OK," Hope replied.

"I doubt if you'll get any reception down here in the valley. There is a spot on the mesa—just as you make the big turn to get on to the road to the main highway, that folks go to use their cell phones, it's about a mile or two up the road."

With the paperwork completed, Hope had the day to herself. She thanked Sarah and headed back to her cabin. The morning was still brisk and she realized that even though it was the end of August, she needed a jacket. Back in her cabin, she picked up her cell phone, pulled her ponytail through a black corduroy baseball cap, and grabbed her jacket. She was ready to explore.

The sun reflected off the rock and pebble bed of Snowy Creek. The water was crystal clear, the current still swift from all the rain the night before. It snaked its way down the mountain into the valley, separating the barns and corrals from the main house and guest cabins. Outside the ranch, the road began a steep climb away from the valley, twisting and turning through thick pines and jutting rocks. Hope enjoyed the morning walk. The scent of evergreens mixed with fresh mountain air and sunshine filtering through the tall trees was invigorating, and even though she was in fairly good condition, she could feel a bit of strain in her breathing and her leg muscles.

She walked on for thirty minutes before the trees naturally thinned and the view suddenly opened up. Ahead was a flat grassy area, about the size of two football fields, standing guard over valleys dotted with groves of trees, herds of horses and cattle. To the north were stunning vistas of snow-capped mountains reaching up to the sky. The colors were brilliant and the contrast of white-capped mountains against the intense blue sky made her stop and stare in awe. Goose bumps raced up her arms and neck at the sight—this was breathtaking!

The wind picked up as she walked toward the center of the mesa. The beauty and grandeur of the view seemed to be intensified by the haunting, eerie howl of the wind. It was magnificent and spectacular. It was overpowering and humbling. Never before had she experienced such perfect beauty. She knew now why Brian had dreamed of them spending time in Wyoming.

Tears welled in her eyes and streamed down her cheeks. Emotions that she had repressed for years exploded with a vengeance. She fell to her knees and for the first time since Brian's death, she wept. She cried out loud and finally allowed herself to grieve—not only for Brian, but for her Dad too, and for all that their senseless murders had stolen from her life.

CHAPTER 5

SOMETHING ABOUT THE accident scene wasn't right. Calder kept replaying last night over and over in his mind. But every time Hope came into the picture, his mind would drift, and he'd loose his train of thought. Damn her, he'd always prided himself on being able to think back and walk through the events of an accident or crime scene and pick up clues with a clear vision of the area. Something about the scene last night told him it was more than an accident, but he couldn't get beyond running into Hope, and feeling her melt into his arms. He wanted to take care of her, but she obviously wanted none of that. She reacted to his badge like a vampire reacts to a cross. He'd have to find out what that was all about. Damn—he was thinking of her again. Maybe a change of scenery would help.

He picked up his keys and jacket and headed out of his mountain home. Jake, a big square-headed black lab, bounded from the shadows of the barn and jumped into the back of the truck into his kennel.

"You don't miss a trick, do you boy?" Calder spoke to the dog in a friendly upbeat voice. The kennel was missing a door, but Jake knew that when Calder got into the truck, it was his job to assume the down, stay position inside the kennel. "We're going to go do some detective work—you ready?" Jake barked a response and his thick tail enthusiastically banged against the wire crate. "And if you behave, I'll introduce you to a fine looking woman over at Snowy Creek." The dog barked again, urging Calder to get a move on.

Beams of morning sun lit the way down the dirt and gravel drive onto the main road. A quick trip down the highway brought Calder to the accident scene. The untrained eye would never know a tragic accident had occurred there the night before. But as he pulled in to the area, he noticed several sets of skid marks on the road. With camera and notepad in hand, he got out of his truck. Jake climbed out of his kennel, bounded from the truck and joined his master's side.

Calder walked back to the road and began taking pictures at different angles, making notes about each shot. He measured the skid marks and jotted dimensions in his notepad. They walked along the side of the road, down away from the accident scene then turned around. "Just as I thought buddy," he said, lifting his hat to run his fingers through dark curly hair. "Look at those skid marks, they overlap in places. This was no accident Jake—someone intentionally ran that lady off the road." Jake wagged his tail in agreement and the pair headed back up to the truck.

Calder took a few more pictures of the accident scene. He walked the same path he had the night before, jotting down everything that came back to him. Staring down at bits of broken glass and pieces of metal mixed with dirt and stone, something red caught his eye. Was it blood? Bending down, he carefully brushed away debris to uncover a cigarette butt, covered in red lipstick. Careful not to touch it with his hand, he picked it up with a twig and flipped it into a plastic bag.

His mind was keen again, on target allowing him to focus on the details. Clues fell into place. He recalled the trunk of the car being open, with luggage and clothing strewn around. "She must have hit that rock with one heck of an impact to pop open the trunk *and* suitcase," Calder thought out loud, and made a note to go into town later and check out the car that had been removed to the impound lot in Buffalo.

He finished up at the accident scene, loaded Jake, and drove back up the highway to the turnoff for Snowy Creek Ranch. Calder's thoughts shifted toward his chance meeting of Hope. Had his meeting with a quarter horse breeder outside Salt Lake taken any longer he would have missed that flight, which would have meant that the deputy would have gotten the call to the accident scene. Chances are he might never have met Hope. But he had. And when he reached out to her, and touched her hand, her dark blue eyes pierced through him like a thunderbolt. It had been a long while since any woman had such an effect on him. It was distracting, but damned enjoyable, and with any luck, he'd find out exactly what it was about her that was so intriguing.

The truck maneuvered the rocky road to the ranch and as he approached the turn at the mesa, his eye caught something on the ground. "Probably a dead animal," he mumbled to himself, but that didn't make sense unless it had been attacked. Animals always found a sheltered, quiet place to die. And he hadn't heard of any mountain lions this far down in quite a while. Then he noticed denim. What would a pile of clothes be doing in the middle of the mesa? He pulled off the road, turned off the truck and went to investigate. Jake joined him and quickly eyed their destination, racing and barking all the way toward the object on the ground.

A barking dog startled Hope back to reality. Before she could get up Jake had crossed the mesa and bounded into her. As he sniffed and licked her face, she quickly realized there was nothing to fear; the dog was just being playful. He continued to jump around excitedly and bark as she wiped the tears from her eyes and took stock of the situation, and not a moment too soon. Calder was in close pursuit!

She quickly got to her feet and brushed herself off. "So, what . . . are you the Dog Catcher too?" she quipped, trying to conceal the fact she had been crying. Jake danced back and forth between Hope and Calder, excited to be playing a new game.

"Are you all right? What in the world are you doing out here in the middle of the mesa?" he asked, scanning her face. Her eyes glistened and her cheeks were as red as her flannel shirt.

"If you must know, I came out here to place a call," she said holding her phone up in front of his face. "And . . . and . . . I couldn't hear because of the wind so I thought it would be better if I crouched down," she added quickly, trying to come up with a believable excuse, other than the truth.

"Well, I didn't mean to interrupt your call. It's just that from the road I thought you were a dead animal, so I stopped to investigate."

"A dead animal? Gee thanks." She knew she probably looked a mess from crying, but a dead animal?

"No. I didn't mean that you looked like a dead animal—it's just that from the road I couldn't tell who or what was out here. And I sure as heck didn't expect to find you all the way out here. I thought you'd still be sleeping!" Calder tried his best to correct the damage his first statement had made, but from the look on Hope's face, he realized he wasn't making points.

"And just what leads you to believe I'd sleep away the day? Is it that I'm from the city or is it because the events of yesterday were a bit too much for a little woman to handle?" She squared her shoulders, lifted her chin and looked straight into his coal black eyes, trying to pick a fight. That seemed to be her only defense to the feelings that crept over her whenever he appeared.

Calder took a step closer and grabbed her by the shoulders—they were within inches of each other. His voice remained calm but the taught muscle in his cheek conveyed his impatience. "I'm not going to play your games

Hope, and I'm not going to fight with you. But if you need to know, it's several hours earlier out here than where you live. And yesterday was a difficult day, for you, for Justin, for me, but *most* of all for our Jane Doe who is lying in a coma in the hospital. I had planned on getting a statement from you and Justin later today, but after my trip to the accident scene this morning, I thought I'd better come by now, because I'll probably be tied up the rest of the day." His eyes searched Hope's as he spoke, trying to figure out what made this woman tick. What was it about him that rubbed her wrong? Why was she acting like such a spoiled brat? And then it clicked as he took in the total picture. Her red cheeks and watery eyes weren't from the wind. She had been crying, and was on the verge of tears again. That's why she reacted the way she had—she was embarrassed for him to see her crying.

"You've made your point, Calder," she said in a sharp, defensive voice. She shrugged his hands off her shoulders and turned away. "I don't want to play games either—I'm tired of that too." She turned back to face him with a look of defiance mixed with pained confusion.

He hurt her and he knew it. Calder couldn't believe how far off he had been in reading her. How could he have been so cruel? Usually his first perception was right on target—but with Hope it seemed his rational thought process was overshadowed. When she was near, all he could think of was touching her, holding her close, and tasting her gorgeous mouth. Any rational thoughts disappeared.

Neither moved nor spoke. Both stood their ground, eyes locked, waiting.

With one step, he was next to her and pulled her into his strong arms. Warm breath tickled his cheek; her scent of lavender enticed him. Unable to resist her nearness, he slowly lowered his mouth on hers. Her lips were soft and tender at first touch.

"No. Stop," Hope whispered as she pulled away, but remained in his embrace. "This isn't right, I can't . . ." she stumbled for words as he held her near. Her body was screaming with desire but her mind was flashing red warning flags. She didn't know which to listen to, but it seemed as though the red flags were winning. She couldn't allow herself to get involved with him—he's a cop—he lives in the middle of nowhere—and this is not what she came here for. She wanted to simplify her life, not make it more complicated. "No," she said, this time with conviction in her voice.

Calder released his hold on her; his eyes narrowed with concern as he studied her.

"I can't do this. This is only going to lead to trouble." Hope stepped back and bit her lip. She avoided eye contact. "I think you'd better go."

"I'm sorry, I shouldn't have . . ."

"No, please don't apologize. Just go."

He cocked his arms on his hips and studied her like she was a puzzle he needed to solve. His instincts told him she needed to talk, but he decided against trying to push the issue, at least for now. "Can I give you a ride back to the ranch?" he asked as Jake reappeared by his side.

"Why don't you go and talk to Justin. I'd like to finish my call. I'll be along shortly."

"I can wait in the truck for you. It's a long walk . . ." Even though it would be hard for him to be so close to her again, he was hoping he could talk her into going back into town to look over the wrecked car. She had witnessed the fresh scene, and he wanted to sort out some questions that had been running through his mind.

"No. You go and talk to Justin. I'll make my call and walk back; I'll be along shortly."

Calder agreed, deciding that after what just happened, this was probably not the best time for him to be persistent. He'd talk to Justin, get a cup of coffee, and then talk with Hope. But what he really needed was a cold shower.

She watched the pair walk across the mesa to the truck; snow capped mountains glistened in the background. "You didn't introduce me," she yelled after them.

He turned to her, a broad grin spread across his face. "His name is Jake, and he was happy to meet you," he said, reaching down and giving his big dog a friendly rub on the head. Calder turned back and continued on to the truck. "Well, at least *you* made an impression," he joked, as Jake wagged his tail and followed happily along.

CHAPTER 6

HER BROTHER'S VOICE was music to her ears. It had been months since Hope had talked with Cliff and she knew he would be surprised to find out she was in Wyoming at a dude ranch. He answered on the barn phone—he was out feeding the horses. For some reason Hope kept forgetting about the difference in time zones. He teased her about riding Western and to watch out for the cowboys. She was tempted to tell him about the wreck and mention Calder, but decided not to. After making certain he had the ranch's phone number in case of an emergency, they said goodbye.

Standing in the middle of the mesa with the sun's golden rays warming her face, Calder's kiss kept flashing in her mind—that warm, wonderful moment. She had no idea that he even *wanted* to kiss her—she had tried to make him angry, and for a moment thought she had. But somehow, he saw right through her. It's as though he read her mind. He knew she was bluffing; he knew she had been crying, and reached out to comfort her with the tenderness of a kiss.

The hike back to the ranch was quick. Return trips were always quicker—it had always seemed to take more time traveling to somewhere new, than it did to return. At the start of a journey every twist and turn in the road, every road sign, she gave her full, undivided attention—very much the same with relationships. In the beginning, every word, every touch, was embedded in the journey of romance. But somewhere during the relationship, the environment becomes routine, and the road signs are ignored. Hope continued to ponder her 'the return is quicker' theory as she walked past familiar rock formations and craggy old trees, back down to the valley and the ranch.

Curious horses raised their heads at the sound of Hope unlocking the ranch gate. They kept a watchful eye on her as she walked down the dirt road toward the corral. A few were interested enough to slowly meander over to her, nosing around for carrots or other treats. She scratched a forelock and ear through the fence, and spoke in a soft voice to the gentle giants. The smell of horses was like perfume to her, arousing a sense of freedom laced with adventure.

The sound of a truck coming down the road from the ranch caused her to turn away from the horses and watch as it turned in to the corral. Dust billowed up around the black pick-up as it pulled to a stop. The window lowered and Calder stuck his head out. "Hey," he called to Hope over the rumble of the diesel engine. "I just got a call and have to head back into town. I'll be back tonight for the Welcome party, could I take your statement then?" He seemed to be all business. Gone was the tenderness Hope remembered from the mesa. It was probably better this way.

"Yes. Sure. I'll see you then." Hope replied. She tried to be upbeat but was a bit disappointed. She had hoped that after taking her statement today, Calder might be available to show her around—she disliked always being on her own. Now she'd have to investigate her new surroundings alone.

She watched as he backed up the big truck and drove off, leaving a dust trail behind. Climbing down from the rail of the corral, Hope decided to head back to the cabin, read through the ranch information, and plan her day from there. If all else failed, spending the day reading a good romance novel on the front porch sounding inviting. The sun had burned off the morning chill—it was turning out to be a beautiful day.

*

The Saloon was bustling when she arrived, country music greeted her ears and the aroma of Mexican food filled the air. Wearing a cobalt-blue turtleneck that matched her eyes, snug black jeans and matching jean jacket, Hope was comfortable with her look. From a quick glance around the room, most everyone else had on similar attire. It appeared that jeans were the little black dress of the west.

This was so difficult. Walking in to a room full of strangers was one of her biggest challenges. From childhood, shyness taunted her—it was an enemy she battled all her life. And ever since Brian died it seemed worse. She was always the third wheel. Holidays were the most difficult—everyone seemed to travel in pairs. She shuddered just thinking about it. That's why her happy-hour buddies were so shocked that she would even think of going to a dude ranch, alone.

She took a deep breath and ventured inside.

According to Sarah, the Saloon was one of the original ranch buildings, dating back to the early 1800s. The logs of the Saloon were all hand hewn, and as such, were not as symmetrical as those in the cabins that came from log cabin kits. Even the chinking was different, it was darker in color. No telling what it was made of.

Appetizers of chicken wings, cheese and crackers, fruit, barbequed mini-sausages, and veggies blanketed the buffet table. At the other end of the Saloon, Justin hopped back and forth behind the bar serving up beer and margaritas. Nearby coolers contained soda, lemonade, water and iced tea for the younger ones and those who preferred a lighter touch.

Deciding to skip the appetizers, Hope headed for the safety net of her new friend. Justin winked as she approached; his sandy hair was slicked back, giving him an appearance of an old-time saloonkeeper. His white apron was folded in half and tied high up onto his chest. A white shirt and string tie completed the outfit.

"Boy if you don't look the part," Hope commented as she pulled out a tall bar stool. "This is really neat in here, it's just like the old saloon's in the western movies." "Yeah! Butch Cassidy and the Sundance Kid might come walking in any minute. Actually, their old stomping grounds aren't too far from here, and this building dates back to their time. You never know, they could have been right where you're sitting!" Hope was beginning to realize that Justin enjoyed spinning yarns. After his tale of Spirit Rock and then coming upon the accident, it wouldn't have surprised Hope in the least to see Butch and Sundance, or their spirits, come strolling in.

She ordered a drink and began talking with a vibrant, athletic looking couple sitting to her left. John and Susan were from Florida, and she quickly learned that their first love was water sports, but they had always been interested in the old west and decided it was time to experience it. They made small talk about the ranch, what brought them to Wyoming, and their skill, or lack of it, around horses. Susan had ridden as a child but John was a bit leery of the whole experience, but was willing to give it a try. Hope enjoyed their conversation and began to relax as the saloon continued to fill.

By the time Sarah and Sam came in, about sixty guests milled about enjoying the social. Sam stopped the music long enough to welcome everyone and provide a bit of ranch history. He was tall, with piercing gray eyes, mostly gray hair and a mustache. He too was wearing a string tie on a western cut blue shirt that matched Sarah's blue western skirt. Together, the owners of Snowy Creek made a strikingly handsome couple.

Sam introduced his ranch hands and the wide range of duties they perform, everything from breaking horses to kitchen duty and housekeeping. Most of the hands were young men and women, just out of college and from all over the country. Next, he turned the activities over to Sarah who quickly got everyone organized and introduced. Hope was surprised at the large number of extended families that vacationed together. She was also relieved to see a few singles in the group. After a brief outline of the variety of daily activities and ranch rules, dinner was served.

Sarah and her crew had cooked up a wondrous display of chicken enchiladas, black bean chili, tacos, chili rellenos, and salad, all set out buffet style. Hope fell in line behind her new friends, Susan and John, and joined them at a round dining table. A guest that Hope recognized as one of the singles in the crowd joined them. Her name was Angela, and she was dressed to kill wearing skin-tight, embroidered, black leather jeans tucked inside black cowboy boots with silver stitching. A blouse of pink silk with fancy black stitching across the bodice completed her outfit. Her dark red hair was pulled back into a bun covered with black netting. She looked like she just walked out of a western boutique. She was very attractive, but a bit garish for the occasion.

"Did I remember you saying you are from Atlanta?" Hope asked, trying to strike up a conversation.

"Well, I'm not really from Atlanta but I live there now. I work for a law firm," Angela said, as she picked at her salad. "And I'm not really here by myself either," she added, her perfectly made up eyes widened as she spoke, giving her an almost theatrical appearance. "I'm surprising my boyfriend, Roger. He's a partner in the firm. He's bringing his son out here for vacation. I thought I'd be here to keep him company while the little guy plays Lone Ranger!" she said, giggling as though they should be in awe of her clandestine idea.

Hope looked up and caught Susan's eye; apparently they were both thinking the same thing—Angela is a bit over the top.

"I thought Roger would be here by now, he and his son flew into Salt Lake the other day. He rented an SUV and wanted to do some sightseeing with his son before driving to the ranch. He's getting a divorce and felt he needed to make things right with the little guy—you know . . ." Angela kept talking, whether any one else at the table was interested or not.

"Geez, does she ever shut up?" Susan asked after she and Hope excused themselves and headed to the bar for a refill. "I hate leaving John there by himself, but he has a way of tuning people out. Maybe she'll get the hint and leave."

"I sure hope so. Can you imagine, that poor little boy? Dealing with his parents' divorce, thinking he and his dad are sharing some special time, and then the girlfriend shows up? She has got to have a screw loose, I can't imagine what her boyfriend is going to think when she "surprises" him." Hope added as they refilled their drinks and made their way back to the table to rescue John.

Across the room, Hope noticed Sam glance outside and then leave. A few minutes later he walked back in with Calder by his side. The brunette who had met him at the airport was nowhere to be seen. Hope wondered if that was by chance or on purpose. She sat on the other side of the room watching the tall cowboy as he interacted with Sam, Sarah and the guests in that area. He looked like he should be in a Polo ad, wearing blue jeans, a crisp white oxford shirt, and brown corduroy jacket with leather trim that was tailored to accent his broad shoulders and narrow waist. He moved around the room with an air of confidence, relaxed and in his element, reflecting his surroundings—rugged, strong, and true.

The music started playing again and some of the crowd migrated toward the dance floor. A ranch hand called out instructions for the two-step as couples glided around. Susan tugged at John, coaxing him onto the dance floor, leaving Hope alone with Angela, who by now was well on her way to being drunk. Through slurred speech she continued to rattle on about Roger and her plans for their wedding. From the few questions that Hope managed to get in, she wondered if Roger knew about the wedding or if it was all in Angela's imagination. Hope also wondered if she got as obnoxious as Angela when she had one too many. If nothing else got resolved from this vacation, she knew she'd always think of obnoxious Angela every time she considered having another drink.

The music changed and shifted to a ballad. She wanted to keep her eye on Calder but didn't want him to see her looking, especially during a slow song, so she excused herself from Angela and went back to the bar looking for Justin. She knew she could count on her new friend for a good laugh or two. And from that angle she could keep her eye on Calder without being obvious. Sam and Sarah were making their way around talking with all the guests, and Calder was deep in conversation with an older couple that was honeymooning at the ranch. The music filled the room with a feeling of romance, a feeling that, since Brian, had always brought with it a twinge of envy and discomfort. In her mind, she was dancing too.

"You look lovely this evening Miss Hanson."

The voice came from behind and surprised her. In a blink of an eye Calder had moved from across the saloon to standing behind Hope. She turned and smiled up at him; even sitting on a tall bar stool he towered over her.

"Well, hello," Hope replied, "When did you get here?" she asked, hoping he hadn't noticed her watching him. She was unsure of herself and didn't quite know what to say. After their meeting on the mesa she wasn't sure how he would react to her. One minute she's arguing, then she's kissing him, then she's telling him to leave—and with little or no explanation. He must think she's a real ditz reacting like that. Then again, maybe he's chalking it up to hormones. That was always what the guys at home said.

"You were right about Sarah—dinner was unbelievable! Did you get to eat?" She was nervous, and didn't know what to say, she felt like she was stumbling over her words.

"I'm not really hungry. But I'm sure I'll be able to talk Sarah into a doggie bag before I leave."

"There's something you said earlier that's been bothering me all day." Hope said, recalling there was quite a bit that was bothering her about the day. She hadn't been kissed like that in years!

"You referred to the accident victim as Jane Doe. Didn't she have ID on her?"

"As a matter of fact, no. That's one of the things I wanted to talk with you about after I take your statement. If you have time now, maybe we could move upstairs where it's a little more private." Calder said, and pointed toward the stairs that ran behind the bar and to a large open loft with sofas and chairs.

Hope shot him a coy glance and asked, "Is it safe?"

His eyes narrowed indicating she had hit a nerve. "Don't worry, I don't go where I'm not invited," he replied, annoyed at himself for falling into her trap. What was it about her that continued to hit that nerve? Were all city women the same?

Making a wide sweeping gesture with his arm, he directed Hope from the barstool to the stairs, walking just far enough behind to realize he had been right. Her long blond hair was swept away from her face and held in place by combs; soft curls cascaded down her back, highlighting all the right curves. She looked great in jeans, and as they climbed the stairs he smiled at his chivalry. If she knew he was enjoying the view from behind she'd be mad, real mad.

They moved across the room to a corner sofa and table. Calder pulled out his notepad and pen and rested his elbows on his knees as he took notes. "Tell me everything you remember from the moment you came up on the accident." He was certain that Hope's statement would match Justin's, but was hoping that she may have noticed that one small detail that could turn into a clue he needed to follow.

"I've worked in a busy trauma unit in a major hospital in Atlanta. I've seen just about everything, so I can't say there was anything odd about the accident. The car ran off the road and hit a boulder head on—the car was an accordion and the lady inside was near death. She was unconscious when we got there. If she survives, she's one hell of a fighter." Hope leaned back in the chair and watched as Calder scribbled notes.

"Do you remember passing any other vehicles on the road that night?"

"No. None. As a matter of fact it was rather eerie driving all the way from Buffalo and never passing another car. That never happens at home."

"What about the car and surrounding area," Calder urged. "Close your eyes and tell me what you see."

"I don't have to close my eyes to describe what I saw."

"I know that," Calder stated. "But I'm asking you to close your eyes and tell me what you *see*. Oftentimes folks will *see* things with their eyes closed that they would have omitted if just describing what they saw. Trust me, it's true," he added, his gaze moved from his notepad to Hope. "Close your eyes Hope." He watched as she slowly closed her eyes and sat quiet.

"Clothes. The trunk and suitcase are open, and clothes are hanging out of the trunk. It looks wrong." Her eyes popped open. "You're right Calder. I don't think I would have noticed how odd that was. It's like someone was digging through the suitcase. But who would do that and not call an ambulance?" Her mind was working fast now, and the questions poured out. "Do you think someone went through her things looking for money?"

"Someone went through her things, but if they wanted to steal they overlooked quite a bit of cash. The only thing I can't find is her identification. She's the only one who can tell us her name and what happened, and so far, she's not saying a word." Calder folded up his notepad and put it back in his coat pocket. "Thanks Hope, I needed to make certain that the clothes were hanging out of the trunk from the beginning, and didn't occur because you were looking for a blanket or something." He eyed Hope for a few minutes saying nothing; a muscle in his cheek that ran down to his scar tightened. "I won't bother you anymore. Enjoy the party!" he said with a hint of sarcasm as he quickly stood, then disappeared down the stairs.

CHAPTER 7

THE NEXT MORNING the Dining Hall was buzzing and people filled the long wood tables. Little ones proudly displaying new cowboy boots and hats could barely contain their excitement at breakfast. Hope spotted John and Susan at a table by the door; they motioned for her to join them.

"Can you believe it? I just offered my services and my own husband turned me down," Susan said, laughing as she told Hope that John had graciously refused her offer to teach him to ride.

"Let's just say I think our marriage will benefit from this brief separation, and you'll have a lot more fun. Chuck has volunteered to work with me today and promises that I'll be ready for the all-day ride Thursday." John winked at Susan and added, ". . . that is if you'll be able to keep up with me!"

Chuck, the head wrangler, visited each guest during breakfast, discussing their riding ability and matching activities to accommodate everyone's needs. Some groups were meeting in the riding ring, while others were going on short trail rides to get acquainted with their mounts. Susan and Hope were glad to hear that they would be riding together with a small group up to Fan Rock.

After breakfast, the girls headed down to the corrals. Responsible for retrieving and storing their equipment each day, the tack room filled as guests scurried about learning where saddles and bridles were stored. And from the look on many faces, they were surprised at the weight of the western saddles and pads. Long yellow slickers were tied with rawhide laces to the back of each saddle; in the mountains, you never know when a storm may pop up. Horses were led out of the corral and stood patiently at hitching posts as guests were instructed in how to groom their mount before saddling. Tails swished back and forth in a lazy cadence as they went through their routine. The first morning was all about instruction.

Hope ended up with a leggy bay gelding named Roman. A quick turn in the riding ring to insure a good match of horse and rider helps Hope adjust to the bulky western saddle. Wranglers tighten girths and adjust stirrups until everyone is comfortable, and ready to hit the trail.

Hope, Susan, and the rest of their small group wound back through the ranch, offering Hope a slightly different view. Sitting atop Roman, the ranch and cabins didn't seem as spread out as when she first arrived. The sound of horses' hooves clip-clopping on the dirt road was music to her ears—and she felt herself exhale and relax into the saddle. Tension exited her body and mind with each melodic step. They rode single file down the cabin road but once outside the compound the trail widened and Hope reined Roman next to Susan's horse, a paint named Flying Spot.

"What do you want to bet that guy on the buckskin with the little boy is Roger?" Hope asked her new friend.

"Yeah, he could be. Definitely fits the description—good looking, light brown hair, and we didn't see them last night at the party." Susan replied. "Do you think he knows Angela is here?"

"Are you kidding? She was probably camped out on his deck waiting for him!" They laughed at the thought of Angela pitching a tent on Roger's deck as the wrangler motioned them forward. The trail opened up and they broke into a gallop across the meadow toward Fan Rock. With the sun in her face and the wind in her hair, Hope felt a happiness and freedom that had avoided her for far too long.

They rode on trails that wound through magnificent tall pines, their spindly branches reaching up to the big vast sky, and crossed crystal clear streams that were so vividly pure that they looked cold. The man she assumed to be Roger was a good rider and kept close to the boy who was obviously enjoying himself. They emerged from a wooded trail into a small meadow, with a wagon and hitching posts and dismounted. They had been riding for over an hour and it was time for a stretch.

The man slid off his horse and then turned to assist the boy.

"What are we stopping for?" the young boy asked. The bridge of his nose was blanketed with freckles. His hat hung loose down his back.

"I thought this would be a good spot to stretch, get a drink of water, and if anyone needs to take a break, I thought I'd point out the fact that there is a rather nice out house over there," the wrangler replied. "What's your name son?"

"I'm Joe, and this is my dad, Roger." His big smile displayed a gap where a tooth had recently been. "We came out here to be real cowboys for a week," he said with pride, throwing out his little chest and grinning at his dad.

"You're a pretty lucky guy," Hope responded, "to have your Dad bring you all the way out here to Snowy Creek so you can be a cowboy."

"Yeah, and my mom's coming too. She'll be here Friday," he said excitedly.

Hope and Susan exchanged quick glances, and then looked at Roger. No reaction. Maybe he didn't know Angela was here; or maybe Angela got so drunk last night she's nursing a hangover and doesn't know Roger arrived. Or maybe Roger was just good at being discreet.

As the riders stretched and enjoyed their break, the wrangler talked of the history of Fan Rock and the surrounding mountain area. That part of the country was a favorite haunt for gunslingers and outlaws of the old west. He spoke of the Hole in the Wall gang and how they probably rode through the very area they were standing on to get to their hideout. Joe's eyes grew larger with each story. He was hooked.

Hope leaned against the wagon, taking in the atmosphere. This was good, and it was fun—more fun than she remembered having in quite some time. Maybe it was the fresh air.

"So who was the good looking cowboy you were talking to last night?" Susan had waited until they were back on their horses and heading back to the ranch. "He didn't stay very long; is he a guest?"

Hope waited for a moment before answering, wondering how much she should share with her new friend. "He's a friend of Sam and Sarah's. I met him on the plane, and on the long ride to Buffalo."

"He sure is a cutie, too bad he's not staying here. He'd be something to write home about!"

Yes, Hope agreed with that. He was something to write home about. Dark curly hair, broad shoulders, tall, and with a voice that could charm the pants off her. Literally. He was perfect, except for that one thing—he was a cop. And there was no way Hope was ever going to get involved with another cop. Always thinking that today may be their last day—always worried that each call could be their last. It had happened with her Dad and had happened again with Brian. She vowed to never again get hurt by a cop, no matter what.

One thing that had always bothered Hope was how Brian wouldn't talk to her. She wasn't sure if he just didn't want to share the details of his cases, or if he was afraid of getting her involved, of worrying her too much. And then there was the standard line her Dad had always used with her mom—she wasn't a cop—she couldn't understand. One thing Hope did understand was being shut out of Brian's world. Maybe if he had shared more, he would still be here.

Calder a cop—go figure . . . Of all the cute guys to meet up with on vacation why in the world did she meet him? But something about Calder was different; maybe it was the location, the small town atmosphere opposed to the city. Calder actually wanted her input. Brian had never talked about a case. Never. It had to be because she was a witness, the first, or second, to arrive on the scene, and had nothing to do with wanting her opinion.

Which reminded her of Jane Doe—maybe she could get a ride into town later to check on the patient. She felt a sense of responsibility toward her, and hoped that she would soon regain consciousness so they could contact her family. It scared her to think that that if something happened to her, no one at home would know, or even be concerned for two weeks. That Jane Doe could just as easily be her, with no one realizing she was in trouble—no one looking for her. Not for a long time. That was scary.

The riders circled Fan Rock, rode the ridge, and then picked up the same trail back to the ranch. As the group rode single file on Cabin Road into the ranch, Hope spotted a black pickup with a dog kennel in the back parked in front of the office. Was he here on business or pleasure, and would he come by to see her? He ran off quicker than she liked, but maybe it was for the best. Every time he was around she had a battle with her senses. Something about his presence scared yet comforted her. He was more than just easy on the eyes; he had a way of connecting with her, of knowing what she needed.

She had come out here to get away from it all, to clear her head, and what had she done but spend most of her first ride thinking about Calder! If she weren't sitting on top of a horse she'd kick herself!

*

Hope, Susan, Roger and Joe left the barn together. They enjoyed their morning ride and were making plans to meet again later in the afternoon to go up on to the other side of the ridge, toward the mesa. Joe skipped ahead to watch a new foal romp in the pasture, as the adults ambled back toward the saloon and cabins. Hope pulled her hat off her head and released her hair from her ponytail. Her fingers ran through it like a comb—it felt so good to let her hair down. Crossing the bridge that connected the road between the barns and the cabins, they stopped to look at the fish swimming in the creek.

"Hey Joe—look at all the fish in the creek," Roger called back to his son. The boy jumped off the pasture fence and raced to his dad.

"Wow, those are pretty big. Do you think we could go fishing too?" Joe was having trouble deciding what to do first. His excitement was contagious.

"We can do whatever you want buddy—fish, ride, learn how to rope cattle, but right now we need to grab some lunch."

Hope watched with pleasure as father and son interacted; they were truly having a good time. Turning back toward the ranch, she noticed Angela standing at the top of the hill by the saloon, arms crossed in front of her chest, looking quite upset. She tugged at Susan's shirt to get her attention, causing Roger to turn and look too.

"Can you and Susan take Joe up to the dining room for me? I need to talk to someone." Roger obviously didn't want Joe to be around when he talked to her. Hope and Susan jumped on the cue to protect the little guy.

"I'll race you," Hope said excitedly, trying to get Joe's mind off his dad. "First one to the top of the hill wins!" Joe took off running up the hill with Hope and Susan in close pursuit. Once inside the dining hall, they found a table on the other side of the dining room so that Joe couldn't see his Dad and Angela.

Roger joined them a short time later, a look of concern on his face; he ate very little lunch.

*

Calder sat in the sun reviewing his notes. Still nothing on Jane Doe's prints—seems she led an uneventful life, at least as far as breaking the law or working in a job requiring a security check. And the VIN number from the car was still being processed. That could take a while, some car rental companies respond right away, others don't look at the alert sheets until they come up short. He'd give his friends in Salt Lake another call; maybe they could spare someone to work the phones and call the new rental car companies.

If only she would regain consciousness, because as far as his gut feeling went, this was attempted murder. He couldn't prove it yet, but he felt certain that the person who ran her off the road and the person who searched her luggage, were one in the same. But who would want to get rid of her, and better yet, why? If her face wasn't in such bad shape from the wreck he'd run her picture in the paper, but it would be some time before the swelling went down and the stitches were removed.

Calder decided to take a chance on Hope returning to her cabin at lunch. The wranglers said she rode out to Fan Rock at nine—it was about a two-hour ride.

Jake's head popped up and his tail began to thump on the wood deck at the sound of footsteps on the stairs.

"Howdy."

Hope stopped dead in her tracks when she saw him. What was he doing on her porch, and why was he always surprising her?

"I had business with Sam and I thought I'd hang around and see if I could talk you into going into town with me. I'm going back to the impound lot to look at the car and I thought two heads would be better than one. Anyways, I think better when there is someone with me to bounce ideas off; no offense Jake."

"Well, I don't know." Hope hesitated trying to find an excuse why she shouldn't go with Calder. She knew *why* she shouldn't go—it was because she didn't trust herself to be near this man. She didn't want to like him and she certainly didn't want to be attracted to him; but she was. Why was he so darn persistent?

"No excuses. I talked to Chuck and he's going to call off all afternoon rides. There is a storm heading our way and he doesn't want anyone out on the trails getting stuck in it."

"A storm? It looks pretty sunny to me. I think your twisting the truth a bit." Hope wasn't sure if he was pulling her leg or not, and didn't want to give in too quick. She bent down to pet Jake and buy time before making a decision. The big black dog took advantage of the situation and rolled on his back, stretching his legs in all directions.

"He has no shame," Calder chuckled, "and always takes advantage of pretty ladies." She noticed how his scar disappeared into a dimple again, becoming a crater anchoring his wide smile.

"Like father like son?" Hope asked as she continued to scratch the big dog's belly and legs. "Labs are great dogs. I had one as a kid; his name was Hunter. He was the smartest, sweetest dog. My mother used him as a four-legged baby sitter—he followed us everywhere!"

"She knew you'd never do anything to jeopardize the safety of the dog—which meant that you'd be safe too. Smart woman."

Hope shaded her eyes to look up at Calder. He had a way of making himself at home wherever he was, enjoying the moment. He was a man who was comfortable in his own skin, and it showed. He wasn't arrogant; he didn't need to be. He expressed confidence in every move.

"Well, I guess I could ask Chuck about the afternoon rides. If he says they're cancelled then I'll go with you. I really don't know how I can help, but I'll try." Hope decided to take a chance. If in fact she couldn't ride this afternoon, it would be a good time to go into town. And maybe she could talk Calder into a trip to the hospital to see Jane Doe.

CHAPTER 8

AT LEAST HE was behaving himself. Calder was being a gentleman and for once, Hope didn't feel as though she had to watch everything she said or did around him and relaxed her guard.

The visit to the impound lot was uneventful. Calder meticulously reviewed the damage to the car, telling Hope more detail than she needed about how the impact of the wreck folded the car into its current accordion shape. Standing there looking at it in the daylight it was difficult for Hope to imagine anyone surviving. The car was virtually demolished. If it weren't for the name Taurus on the rear panel of the car, she would never have recognized the make or model. She focused on the rear end of the vehicle and wondered if the trunk popped open from the impact or if it had been opened after the crash.

"More than likely, the trunk popped open during the wreck. Not directly from the impact, but from when the trunk latch broke. The actions of the cable breaking actually released the trunk latch," Calder stated. She looked at him in amazement—he was reading her mind.

"What?" he asked. He had read her right. He thought that the way she was looking at the trunk she was trying to figure out the mechanics of it opening during the wreck. He could tell by her serious countenance as she looked at the latch and stood back to take in the big picture. He always got a kick out of studying people and anticipating their actions.

"You're timing is impeccable Calder. Did they teach you to read minds in the police academy?" she asked, reaching over to peek under his hat. He flinched and his hat ended up catawampus on his head. "Now that's the way you should wear it—it really adds character," Hope chuckled as she stood back and surveyed him. Dark curls popped out from under the ten-gallon hat providing a contrast to the firm but kind face. He made a goofy face and once again his scar evaporated in his dimples. Hope was loosening up with the playful antics; he really was a nice guy.

"Oh, I almost forgot," he said, "my hand is too big; can you see if you can get to the ashtray, and let me know if you feel anything in it."

"Like what?" she shot him a puzzling glance.

"Don't expect anything will bite you. Just wondering if she was a smoker or not," he added, watching Hope reach down through the wreckage, struggling to find the ashtray.

"Got it."

"A cigarette?"

"No. The ashtray. It's clean—nothing there." She wriggled out of the car and straightened her shirtsleeve. "You know what's funny? It opened up—wasn't even stuck."

She cocked her head and studied Calder's expression, or lack of it. "As you expected?" she asked, trying to figure out the puzzle pieces.

"Just collecting and verifying. Nothing more."

"Nothing more, huh?"

"Nothing more here, but I'd like to take you to the police station now. That is if you don't mind. I need a woman's point of view on something." Calder placed his hand in the small of her back to direct her toward the gate of the impound lot. His touch was comforting, caring. It felt good to be around a man who took charge but didn't demand.

"And after that if there is anything you'd like to see or do, like go to the grocery, I'm all yours." He winked and held the gate open for her to walk through first. A quick whistle brought Jake from behind a row of impounded cars and in one swift leap, into the bed of Calder's truck.

"I might take you up on that. Actually, I'd like to stop by the hospital and check in on our patient."

"Don't trust the local hospitals?" A tone of sarcasm accompanied his comments.

His words stung. Had she acted as though this way of life was below her? Had she become so caught up in her fast life of parties and living high that she came across as better, or more privileged? She glanced at him, trying to figure out if he had really meant to deliver such a low blow.

"I use to be a nurse Calder, and believe it or not I am truly interested in the well-being of that woman." It had been years since she had felt that connection of nurse to patient. Sometimes it was a bond that carried over after her charge was released from the hospital; sometimes it ended with her shift. But it was always there, that bond, that need to help. The hugs, the words of thanks that always brought a lump to her throat. Patients touched her heart; maybe that's why she had to get away after Brian died.

Her heart was too pained for any contact. She hadn't realized how much she missed nursing until now, until she once again was caring for someone in need. Maybe her heart had healed enough to once again offer it. She didn't know—but she did know she had to check on Jane Doe.

"I'm sorry, I'm very protective of our little town, and more times than not if I take an outsider to the hospital they get a look of disbelief on their face, because of the size. It may not be big, but those docs know what they are doing." He reached across the seat for her hand. "That's twice now I've made the wrong assumption about you. I promise, it won't happen again. Forgive me?"

The sarcasm was gone from his voice; his tone now was honest and sincere.

"This time. But just don't let it happen again." She gave him a quick smile and he squeezed Hope's hand before pulling out into traffic.

*

The police station was larger than she imagined, but she wouldn't dare tell Calder that. Not after his earlier comment about the hospital. Yet she had to laugh to herself; she really was expecting it to look like the one in Mayberry. Instead, she entered a very modern building, situated on a corner lot just outside of historic Buffalo. A middle-aged lady with light-brown hair slicked back into a short ponytail sat behind a large modular desk next to a dispatch radio and computer. A small fan perched on top of her computer provided a personal breeze. She looked up with a phone to her ear, grinned and waved when Calder introduced her as Doris. They headed down a hallway to his office, passing by several closed doors. Hope wondered if they were interrogation rooms or other offices.

"Make yourself comfortable, I'll be back in a minute," he said, pointing to a sofa and chair in the corner of his office. It was a corner office with large windows on both walls offering a spectacular view of the mountains. His desk was rather orderly; random stacks of paper occupied desk trays on one corner. A blank computer screen stared out from a large corner credenza. The desk and credenza seemed taller than usual, and a quick glance down indicated why. Phone books were stacked under the legs to raise the furniture to accommodate Calder's long legs. Hope chuckled at the fix.

She crossed the room to look at the gallery of pictures on the wall. Pictures of Calder with Jake as a puppy; a beautiful log home on a lake; an older couple; and one with what must have been his FBI friends all wearing dark suits and ties. Another picture showed Calder, another man, and a beautiful girl with long curly strawberry blonde hair standing between them, all in formal attire, probably taken at a wedding or other black tie event. They were all smiling and the girl was holding out her left hand, flashing a ring.

Hope was deep in thought studying the picture when Calder reentered the room. Jake looked up from his bed by the desk, alert, and always ready to do his master's bidding.

"My sister's attempt to make my office homey," he said nodding his head in the direction of the photos. He placed a large cardboard box on the coffee table by the sofa. "This is everything from Jane Doe's suitcase. I'd like you to take a look at it."

"I don't understand? You've gone through it, haven't you?" Hope peered down at the brown box, half afraid for him to open it.

"Yes but I want a woman's point of view—a city woman."

Piece by piece, Calder removed items of clothing from the box—all high quality, stylish clothes. Brown suede jeans, Ralph Lauren sweaters and jackets, long blue jean skirt, turquoise and silver jewelry among many other accessories. Even the socks and silk undergarments were of the highest quality.

"Well, all I can say is she dresses very well. This is all designer wear, no inexpensive discount items here. I would say that whomever she is she probably is not hurting for money," Hope remarked, remembering some of the items she had seen in the boutiques when she was shopping for this trip. "Those brown suede jeans cost more than most folks make in a week."

"Is there anything else in there?" Hope questioned.

"Just this." Calder pulled out a sealed plastic bag from the bottom of the box. "This is what she had on, and here's a small bag with her jewelry. I was hoping for an inscription in the ring, but no luck."

"What about toiletries and make-up? Wasn't there a make-up bag or hair-dryer? Most women I know don't leave home without them." Hope looked over the items again, wondering what the woman was thinking when she packed. Was she looking forward to her trip? Was it a vacation? Was she meeting someone? Was she on her way home?

"No." Hope blurted out, answering her own question.

"No what?"

"No, she wasn't on her way home. These clothes are all clean. She was on her way somewhere."

"You're right. But where? If I could figure that out I'd have this case half solved. I was hoping that you could give me some insight as to where a lady like this might be going."

"I don't know, but from the looks of her lingerie I would venture a guess that she was meeting someone she wanted to impress." Hope gently ran her hand over the champagne colored silk and lace teddy that lay in front of her. "I'm almost embarrassed to say it but I brought flannel pajamas with me. It gets cold up here at night!"

Calder chuckled at her comment. "But I'm sure you look sexy as hell in those flannels," he added, his dark eyes once again alive with mischief.

"Oh yes, no make-up, hair in a ponytail and flannel pajamas, now that's hot! Only Jake would love me like that." The big dog's head lifted again at the mention of his name. His body molded in the large sheepskin dog bed.

"And his owner," Calder added under his breath as he put the remaining items back in the box. He never could understand why women thought that certain clothes made them sexy. It's the woman who is sexy, not the clothes. It's how she carried herself, the soft look in her eyes and on her face. It's the tenderness and caring in her heart.

"By the look of things outside, we'd better get a move on if we don't want to get stuck in that storm. I'll need to swing by my place and drop off Jake before we head over to the hospital," he said, trying to take his mind off of Hope in her pj's.

As she followed Calder out of the office, Hope took one more quick look at the pictures on the wall. He mentioned a sister. Was the girl with the diamond his sister or . . . ?

*

Calder turned off the main road onto a gravel lane that twisted and turned around massive trees, and into a clearing containing a two-story log cabin with a wrap-around porch overlooking a lake. Off to one side stood a small log barn with a pasture behind it. It was all rustic and manly, yet one of the most charming settings she had seen in years.

"I'll only be a minute." Jumping out of the truck, he was on the porch in just a few long strides. Jake followed obediently.

Hope watched his every move before he disappeared into the cabin. She couldn't help but notice how nicely he filled out his jeans from behind, but she wondered why he hadn't invited her in. Maybe the place wasn't picked up, or maybe someone else was there. She'd never know, but she would have loved a tour of the cabin, half from her interest in real estate, and half just to see how Calder lived. As much as she hated to admit it, he was a very interesting man.

Movement by the barn caught her eye. An elderly man dressed in overhauls held a fishing pole and slowly ambled down a path toward the lake and disappeared beyond the ridge. For a moment, she wondered why anyone would fish in the rain and then she remembered her father saying—'the fish don't care if it's raining.' She smiled at that memory—fishing was one of the few good memories she had of her father. It was the only time she had him all to herself; her mother hated fishing and her brother was more interested in girls.

Raindrops splattered the windshield before Calder got back in the truck. She watched as dark clouds rolled over the mountains.

"Someone headed down to the lake for a bit of fishing," Hope said, wondering who the man was.

"That's my Dad. He goes down there every day this time—rain or shine."

He was serious again, and Hope felt she was intruding. She waited a moment, unsure if she should ask why, and then decided to go ahead. "Every day at the same time? Why is that?"

Calder cocked his head and reflected a few minutes before speaking. "He and my mom loved to come to my lake and fish. Even before the house was built they use to pack a sandwich, come out here, and sit for hours, talking and fishing, fishing and talking, and then just sitting and enjoying each other's company. Just before her death, they made a point of going every day. I guess it's his way of staying connected."

"That is so sad but sweet at the same time. Does he live nearby?"

"He's lived with me for the past year. I'm building an addition on to the cabin—so he'll have his own living area, not just a bedroom. After thirty-eight years I'm finally learning who my Dad is—and I like him."

The man sitting next to her was a lot more complex than she thought the other night when he bounded up the steps of the aircraft in Salt Lake City. Complex and caring—that was a mix she hadn't experienced in years.

Calder drove with one hand on the wheel, maneuvering the truck up the winding mountain road. Before long they rounded the corner of Spirit Rock and both looked in the direction of the accident scene, just in case.

"You wanted to know if Justin and I remembered any other vehicles on the road that night. What about you? You left before we did, did you see anyone?" Hope was back to thinking about the accident. Remembering the brown suede jeans and the champagne teddy that were now being stored in a box—Would Jane Doe ever get to wear them?

He didn't look at Hope when he spoke, but she thought he hesitated before he replied. "I didn't head right home. I was still in Buffalo when I got the call to go to the accident," Calder replied, but offered no further information as to where he was.

She was embarrassed for asking, he was investigating the accident, not her. "Oh," was the only thing she could think of to say. How could she have been so stupid to ask him such a personal question, and why was her mind jumping to conclusions? Just because a beautiful brunette picked him up in his truck—it really didn't mean anything—other than the fact that they knew each other. And apparently he wasn't going to elaborate on where he was or with whom.

"You've got a good mind, that's why I asked for your help today. I appreciate your interest. So don't quit asking."

*

By the time they arrived at the hospital, the bottom had dropped out of the sky. Calder pulled up to the covered entrance to let Hope out without getting drenched, and then he drove off to park. He was surprised Hope had wanted to visit their Jane Doe, but that was before he learned that she had been a nurse. He laughed to himself thinking of how many men must have awakened from surgery to think they had died and gone to heaven. To wake up to that face, soft glistening skin, full lips, and dark blue eyes. And her interest in the case surprised him. She had a very good knowledge of police procedures and terminology; he would have to ask her if someone in her family was in law enforcement.

He entered the small hospital and went directly to the critical care unit, which basically was the room directly across from the nurses' station on the 3rd floor. He spoke with Nancy, the head nurse, all the while watching through the glass windows into Jane Doe's room. Hope stood next to the bed, holding Jane's hand with her left while stroking the top of head with her right hand. If he didn't know better he would have thought she was visiting an old friend, catching up on gossip. But this old friend was still in a coma; yet Hope was there.

"You know, that's her best therapy," the head nurse told Calder. "Unfortunately there aren't enough of us around here to spend the extra time she needs."

"She's a nurse. At least, she used to be."

"Ahhhh . . . she knows then. Does she need a job?—we've got plenty of openings." Head nurse Nancy was always on the lookout for new staff.

"You'll have to ask her. She's from the east—just here on vacation." He didn't like the sound of those words—just here on vacation. What kind of vacation was this? What kind of woman would spend her vacation in a hospital with a woman she didn't even know, and who probably didn't even know anyone was with her? This woman he watched through the glass intrigued him more each day.

CHAPTER 9

THE MORNING WAS cooler than usual. The rain brought in an early chill from Canada. According to Justin, late August could sometimes feel like October. Hope dressed in layers, unsure of what the weather would do. She figured she could always remove a layer or two and tie them around her waist.

The group from yesterday was planning a four-hour trek over to the other side of the ridge, to the flat country as Chuck calls it. Beyond the ridge, plains stretched as far as the eye could see. The perfect place to let the horses open up, and stretch their legs.

The horses were enjoying the cool weather too. They seemed to be excited and ready to get on the trail. Roman danced in place as Hope swung her slim figure up and on the big horse. Susan was having difficulty mounting Flying Spot. At breakfast she admitted she should probably be spending the morning in the hot tub rather than riding again, but Chuck assured her that the best cure for stiff muscles is to use them again. She figured she had sufficiently warmed them up just trying to mount.

"Why don't you go over to the mounting block—it'll make life a whole lot easier," Hope advised her new friend.

"Is that what that is? I wondered why they would have a block of cement sitting there." Susan made it up on her first attempt from the mounting block and trotted over to the other riders. "I think I just found my new best friend. Now if I could only carry it with me—what am I going to do when we stop out there?"

"Don't worry, we'll get you back on board!" Hope laughed as the group guided their horses between barns and around wagons heading for the back trail to the ridge. Roger and Joe trotted up behind them.

"Morning!" Hope called out to the father and son. Her wide smile was usually contagious, but this morning, Joe didn't look too happy.

"What's the matter little guy, I thought you liked to ride?" Hope was trying to get a smile or some response from the little dude, but he wasn't talking. She thought he was about to cry.

"Hey, Joe, Hope is speaking to you." Roger shook his head and sighed, but kept his eyes fixed on his son.

"Good morning," Joe managed to speak in monotone. It was like pulling teeth, but he finally spoke.

"It is a good morning Joe, and you're going to have fun today in spite of yourself. There's nothing like the back of a horse to make everything right." Roman pranced sideways under a tight rein as Hope spoke to Joe and finally got him smiling. She reached over and roughed up his hair. "Now that's the attitude! Cowboys don't worry about anything except their horse. You keep your mind on that little filly and everything will be fine."

Once beyond the barns and out buildings, they cantered along the trail up to the ridge. Steam rose from the horses as they snorted against the cold morning air. The higher they rode the cooler it got; Hope knew it would be a while before she needed to shed any layers.

They made their way across pastures of cattle grazing and soaking up the morning sun. Some of the cattle showed an interest in the riders, their big black eyes watching every move; others paid no attention.

The squeak of leather moving between horse and rider was like a lullaby; almost trancelike in the effect it had on Hope. The scenery was vast and breathtaking. Just being there with no sign of people or cars or power lines for as far as the eye could see was amazingly beautiful. Nature. It can have a powerful effect. She wondered if Calder had ever ridden up here—she'd have to ask him. That is if she ever saw him again. She had looked at the car and clothes; he probably didn't need anything more from her. And he hadn't even mentioned anything about kissing her. Actually, he acted as though he could care less about ever kissing her again. Either he didn't take rejection well or he meant what he said about not going where he wasn't invited. She was reflecting on yesterday's events when Roger trotted up next to her.

"It's beautiful up here isn't it?"

"Yes, it's hard to even think of work, TVs, or the rest of the world. You can really free up your mind out here." Hope had an ethereal look on her face. She felt like a sponge, soaking up the healing effects of her surroundings. Her skin glistened like the morning dew.

"I'm sorry about Joe this morning," Roger said. "He's a bit upset with me."

"About Angela?" Hope questioned. She wasn't going to pry but since he seemed to want to talk about it she thought it was fair game.

"Yes. How'd you know her name?"

"She sat with Susan and I at the reception dinner. She told us all about how she was going to surprise you."

He shook his head; worry was written all over his face. "I don't know how this got so out of hand. I met Angela at the office. One thing led to another and, well, you know the rest of the story. I got involved with Angela but didn't know how to get out of it. It didn't take Judy long to figure out something wasn't right. Then Angela called the house one night looking for me, she was threatening to kill herself if I didn't come over. I did, and when I got back home Judy and Joe were gone. To make a long story short, it's been a hell of a year. We were headed for divorce when I finally woke up and realized what a fool I was. I broke it off with Angela. Judy and I have been talking and are going to try to make a go of it. We were both looking forward to this trip to see if we could get beyond the Angela thing. And here she is." His shoulders looked like he was carrying the weight of the world on them and was relieved to finally talk about the mess he was in. "I've tried to tell Angela that it's over between us, that Judy and I are getting back together, but it's like she doesn't hear a word I say."

"I don't know if I should tell you this or not, but at the reception, she told me all about how you proposed and all the details of the wedding you are planning." Hope was confused, it was his word against hers but after seeing Angela in action, she leaned toward believing Roger.

"What's bad is that Judy is coming here Friday. She had a business meeting this week, or else she would have come out with Joe and I. And I can't get Angela to leave." He spoke in low tones, not wanting Joe or others to hear what he was telling Hope.

"I've been up on the mesa several times trying to call Judy, but all I ever get is her voicemail, and I'm not going to leave a message like that. I've got to reach her in person and tell her not to come; tell her the weather is horrible and not to waste her time coming out."

"What about the truth?"

"I don't think that would work. At this point I'd lose her for good. She still loves me, but doesn't trust me, and if you don't have trust, well . . . I love her more than I knew; I really screwed up." Roger looked tired and concerned, like he was at his breaking point.

"Is there anyone you can call to check on her?" Hope felt sorry for Roger, but even worse for Joe. No wonder the poor little cowboy was so upset this morning!

"No. When she moved out she rented a place in the country. Her nearest neighbor is a mile away and I have no idea of a name, I think Judy wanted it that way. She's a very private person."

"Well if what you're saying about Angela is true, and I'm not saying I don't believe you, I'm just saying that if what you're saying can hold up in court, you should be able to take out a restraining order on her."

"I will once I get back to Atlanta. But that won't help me here, now. I feel as though we're going to have a showdown at the OK corral."

"Well, where is Angela now? How'd you manage to sneak away from her?"

"My only saving grace is she doesn't know how to ride. She's taking lessons from Chuck."

Hope made a mental note to ask Susan about John's beginner group. It would be interesting to see if she is changing her story or if she is planning to stay.

"I wish I could help, but . . ." Hope didn't know what else to say, and thought she already knew more than she needed to about Roger's private life.

"Just keep Joe smiling. This is his dream trip, and now it's turning into a nightmare." They rode for a few minutes in the quiet of the morning. A hawk glided by overhead, probably calling out to its mate.

"Thanks for listening Hope, I'm sorry to have dumped all this on you. For Joe's sake, I felt as though I needed to explain."

Roger loped ahead to join up with Joe; Hope dropped back next to Flying Spot.

"How's it going back here, you doing OK or need a break?" Hope asked Susan, she knew that Susan's legs probably needed a rest.

"Yeah—a break—the hot tub! I'm thinking long and hard about heading back. I don't know if I can last another three hours." Susan laughed and shifted around in her saddle trying to stretch. "But tell me, you and Roger were head to head for quite some time. Did you get the scoop?"

"Did I get the scoop? What a mess. Listen, how about we turn around; I'll ride back in with you and I'll tell you all about it along the way. I'll ride up and let the wrangler know we're going back." Hope nudged Roman into a canter and moved around the group of riders to the wrangler.

After assuring the wrangler they knew their way and saying goodbyes, Hope and Susan started back to the ranch. She had an idea that might help Roger and Joe, and wanted this time with Susan to work through it.

*

Before the accident, Calder drove by the entrance to Snowy Creek every day and never thought twice about it. Now, every time he got near the ranch he found himself wondering what Hope was up to. Was she out riding? Was she a good rider? Should he invite her to go riding with him? Is she hiking or just relaxing in her cabin? Now he needed an excuse to be there, just in case he would see Hope. But he never needed an excuse before to stop in and visit, why should he need one now? No. He had work to do in the office as well as go to the hospital, and needed to stop by the feed store too. He was too busy to accommodate a whim. Yesterday had been difficult enough, spending that much time with her and acting like she didn't drive him crazy. Every time he got near her, or when her scent lingered, he wanted to reach out and pull her to him, to taste her lips and more. But Hope had made it very clear; she wanted no part of him.

Arriving at the office, Doris handed him a stack of messages, but unfortunately, none of them indicated a possible ID for Jane Doe. A phone call to the doctor that morning indicated she had been upgraded to critical but stable condition—still comatose. As long as she remained comatose and with no response from the rental car companies, his investigation was at a standstill. But Calder's background told him that as long as there is a victim, there is a perpetrator. And that perpetrator is still out there, going about routine day-to-day activities. And sooner or later, criminals always make mistakes. That's what Calder was waiting for—the mistake. It would come, and he had to be aware of everything to recognize it.

The rest of the day was routine, and by 3PM, Calder decided to head over to the hospital and check on Jane Doe. Even in a town as small as Buffalo, the hospital always seemed to have business. Unfortunately, people always get sick.

The CCU still had only one patient—Jane Doe.

Nancy was on duty again. As Calder got off the elevator and walked toward her she looked up over the rim of her glasses. "You know, people are going to start talking. How are you doing today Mr. Elliott?" Nancy put her pen down and stood up to talk across the tall nurses unit.

"Good Nancy, how's our patient?"

"Getting more popular by the minute!" Nancy stated matter-of-factly. She motioned toward the patient room—and Calder could see someone sitting by the bed. "The lady you brought by yesterday came back today with a radio and a book. She's been in there reading to her for the past hour. Before that, a lady came in for a few minutes, and then left."

At the mention of Hope, Calder's attention shifted to the room; he focused on her trim form sitting on the edge of the chair next to the bed. She was amazing, she wasn't responsible and . . . .

"What did you say?" Calder's mind focused back on what Nancy was saying.

"I said she's been sitting in there for the past hour reading to her."

"And there was someone else?"

"Yes. A lady came in just after lunch. She didn't stay long."

"A lady? Did she give her name?

"No. She just asked if she could check in on the accident victim. I asked if she knew her. She said no. I thought it was kind of strange but then she said she was with the local paper, so I let her go in. But she didn't stay long, and I never saw her get any paper out or anything." Nancy was concerned at the Police Chief's sudden interest.

"Have you ever seen her before?"

"No."

"Don't you think it odd that if she were a reporter with the paper you would have seen her somewhere around town? Can you describe her to me?" Calder had his pad and pen out. He checked one more time on the glassed-in room. Hope was still reading. Good.

"Describe her. Let me see. She was about my height, that's 5'6", and she had reddish-brown hair. It was stuffed into a cowboy hat but some strands were falling out around her face. I remember I thought it odd that she didn't take her hat off in the hospital, but I didn't say anything."

"And about how old?" Calder was excited. This may have been the mistake he'd been waiting for.

"Oh my, I'm such a bad judge of age. You know, when you get to be my age everyone under 40 looks like a kid!" She chuckled and pulled off her glasses. "I really don't know, but if I had to guess I'd say around 25 or 30. She was rather pretty in a made up kind of way."

"What do you mean?"

"She wore a lot of make-up. Women notice things like that; and around here, women don't wear much make-up. Kids yes, but women? No."

Calder reached across the nurses unit and planted a kiss on the head nurses cheek. "Nancy, you're a doll. Thanks for keeping your eyes open. Until I can get a deputy posted here, I'd like you to call me if anyone comes in here to see her. OK?"

"You bet. I'm glad I can help. And I'll make sure that the other shifts are aware of the no visitor without checking with you policy." She was proud of the fact she could be of help in solving the hit and run, and possibly locate the unknown woman's family.

Calder crossed the unit and leaned against the door of the patient room before knocking lightly. Hope looked up, smiled at him, and continued reading a sentence.

"Excuse me, I have to put the book down for minute and step out of the room. But don't worry, I'll be back," she said, squeezing the hand of the lady who lay still in the hospital bed. Tubes and machines were connected to all parts of her body.

"Hi. What brings you here today?" Hope asked, running her fingers through her hair, and carefully tucking it behind her ear.

Calder had never seen her with her hair totally loose, falling around her face and shoulders, and he watched in awe. It was the color of honey, thick and full, defying her every attempt to secure it behind her ear.

"I thought it was time to check on my girls," he winked at Hope, and she reacted in a way that surprised him. She didn't attack.

"Something's up, I can see it in your eyes. What is it?" Hope said, stepping out of the patient room into the hall with Calder.

"Jane Doe had another visitor today."

"Oh my God, did someone identify her? That's wonderful!" With the excitement, Hope reached up and hugged Calder's neck. "That is such good news, you have no idea how worried I've been about her." She stepped back but they were still holding on to each other's arms.

"Well I hate to say anything that will take you from my arms, but it's not that. I have a feeling it's someone who knows what happened out there the other night. And probably knows who she is." Calder was serious again. "And I'm afraid she's not out of danger. I'm going to post a deputy by her door, 24 hours. No one in or out without my approval."

The excitement she had felt a moment ago was quickly converted to a dull numbness. She just knew someone somewhere had to be looking for Jane Doe.

"So who was here earlier?"

"Nancy said it was a woman, about 5'6", 25-30 years old, with brownish-red hair." He waited a moment and then remembered another descriptor. "Oh, yeah, and Nancy said she was pretty but wore a lot of makeup."

"Well that blows my theory," Hope said. She spoke in low tones, not wanting to share their discussion with Nancy or anyone else on the ward. "I thought for sure she was on her way to meet her boyfriend and the husband ran her off the road. Thus, no husband looking for her." She enjoyed the fact that Calder encouraged her to express her ideas on the case, and didn't scoff at her ideas.

"That's a possibility. But if it was the husband, don't you think he'd file a missing persons, just to take the suspicion away from him?" Calder liked to try on different theories, and now he had a description to use—it was like putting together a jigsaw puzzle. He just had to make certain each clue went in the right spot. "Maybe it was a business partner, someone other than a family member who knew her schedule, and wanted her out of the picture."

"Can't you put that description in to the computer at the Motor Vehicle Department to see how many matches you have?"

"Very good. I've been meaning to ask you, is anyone in your family in law enforcement? You have such a good knowledge of police terms and procedures. That's not common Hope."

"Well, maybe I'm just an uncommon woman," she replied, and looked away from Calder into the patient room.

"That I believe. But I also believe you are avoiding my question. How are you so familiar with police procedures?"

"And if I refuse to answer, what will you do, take me downtown to interrogate me?" she asked, raising her chin in defiance. This was the first time in days she felt as though she was losing ground with him, and the only way she knew to get it back was to pick a fight.

"I'd be careful if I were you. The last time you raised your chin like that to me I kissed you. Is that what you want?"

Calder had turned the tables on her. She felt trapped, if she continued to aggravate him, he'd kiss her, and if she didn't . . . "You know, I don't see how this discussion is helping that woman lying helpless in there. You should be out combing the streets looking for a 5'6 redhead wearing heavy makeup!" A visual was created in her mind's eye as she quoted the description, and it was familiar.

COUNT A HUNDRED STARS

"Wait. Did you say brown hair or red hair?"

"I wrote it down . . . let's see. She said reddish-brown hair. Why?"

"If she would have said red hair, I'd say I know someone who fits that description. She's out at the ranch, and she is looney. She's playing fatal attraction with one of the guests; followed him out here. What's really bad is that his son is so sweet and cute, and there he is messing around with some bimbo."

"She was at the Welcome Reception. I'm surprised you didn't notice her. She was all dolled up in black leather and pink silk."

"Pink silk and black leather—how in the world did I miss that? I'll have to call Sarah and find out about her. What's her name?"

"Angela. I don't know her last name; just Angela. But Sarah would know. Apparently she showed up without a reservation and paid cash for a cabin near Roger's.

"And Roger is?"

"He's the attorney that she's chasing. He and his son Joe are at Snowy Creek on vacation. And his wife is joining them at the end of the week, so he's going nuts trying to figure out how to get rid of Angela before the wife shows up."

"This sounds more and more like a soap opera. Can you tell me more about her on the ride back to the ranch?" Calder asked, unsure of how she was planning on getting back to the ranch, but hoping she would take him up on his offer.

"Well, I've got a cell phone number of one handsome wrangler that's visiting some friends in town. He told me just to call and he'd come pick me up," Hope said, wanting to tease the Buffalo Chief of Police just a bit.

CHAPTER 10

SARAH AND SAM had a large bowl of Tootsie Rolls sitting on the island in their kitchen. The log home had a surprisingly up-to-date interior—similar to the cabins only on a much larger scale. Hope felt a bit ill at ease in their home and wasn't certain why. She was comfortable talking to them in their role of owner of the dude ranch she was vacationing at, but somehow, sitting in the den and socializing with Calder seemed odd.

"I promise you one thing," Sarah said to Calder, "if that girl ever calls to book here again we are full. She is strange. She was in the office earlier today asking me if there was any way she could have a radio phone installed in her cabin because she had business to take care of and the "quaintness" of the ranch was making her life difficult." Sarah took a deep breath to calm herself before she continued. "She then went on about how she had friends in the travel industry and all she needed to do was put out the word and we'd be eating dust." Sarah put her hands on her hips and stood looking between Calder and Sam as though neither believed her. But they both did.

"How'd you get her out of the office?" Sam asked.

"I told her we'd be glad to refund her money for the nights she stayed with us. I didn't want her to be uncomfortable and inconvenienced by the "faux country ambiance" as she called it. Faux country ambiance my eye—we *don't* get reception in this valley, and we haven't found it cost effective or important to bring cable into the ranch," Sarah said adamantly. "And that poor little boy. I can't believe I actually gave her the cabin next to the Longacres, but when she made her reservation I had no idea she was so obsessed or what she was up to."

"But I'm still having trouble making the connection between Angela and Jane Doe, unless it was some freak coincidence on the road." Calder said. Every couple of minutes he would walk over to the tootsie roll bowl and grab a few. He seemed to think better while he chewed. "And there is no law against visiting someone in the hospital, even though I'm sure if she is the one that was visiting Jane Doe, it wasn't to read her a book." Calder winked at Hope, watching her around Jane Doe was like watching a mother with a sick child.

"It could have been road rage," Hope offered, remembering a recent case at home where two women began arguing at an intersection and one chased and then shot and killed the other woman.

"Road rage, on a road seldom traveled? I don't think so." Calder said, trying not to diminish Hope's addition to their brainstorming.

"It was probably just an accident. Maybe someone else came along and stole her purse and ID, or maybe it got thrown out of the car on impact. Maybe the person that stopped to check saw it lying on the ground and in shock from the accident scene, picked it up and took it with them. Maybe now they're too afraid to call or turn it in." Sarah added.

It was possible. All of the suggestions were possible, but probably none were actually what happened.

They visited for a while longer, talking of the upcoming overnight ride and the rooster catching contest for the kids. They left Sam and Sarah's and began walking up the lane towards Hope's cabin. She hadn't invited him but didn't push him away either. She felt like a kid in grade school, with the boy she had a crush on walking her home from class. The closer they got to the cabin the more she hated for their walk to end. The sun was setting and shadows crisscrossed the valley. Pink and blue puffs of clouds drifted into pink and blue wisps as they moved over the valley into the mountains.

Calder propped a hand against the cabin door and looked down at Hope. Her thick golden blonde hair beckoned for him to touch it, to know its texture and to inhale its heady scent. He had to control himself and resist the temptation standing before him. "I have an idea Hope, and I need your help. Can I come in for a few minutes to talk?"

She was going to invite him in anyway, but was glad he asked first. "Only if you make yourself useful and start that fire. That's one thing I haven't mastered yet."

"And as long as I'm around, you don't need to worry about it." He took his hat off and tossed it in the side chair. Rubbing his hands together he went to work, and within minutes, the inviting crackle of a fire filled the room. The small cabin would soon be warm and cozy.

"Would you like a glass of wine?" Hope asked. Not waiting for an answer, she removed two wine glasses from the cabinet, found the bottle of wine and placed them on the coffee table. The environment was starting to scare her, and the fact that she was the one creating it was even scarier. Alone in a cabin with an intriguing, handsome cowboy, a bottle of good wine and a crackling fire—that was danger. But tonight, Hope's warning lights weren't sending their usual message, and she quickly forgot her concern.

Calder leaned against the mantle and poked at the growing fire while surveying the atmosphere. This was a tempting situation. Hope was relaxed and open sitting on the sofa with a glass of wine, almost beckoning him to join her. But he had to watch himself, he didn't want to get her angry or his plan might not work. He picked up his glass of wine and went back to the fire.

"After listening to you and Nancy share descriptions this afternoon, I have to believe that this Angela person may be our mysterious visitor. But I don't want to scare her off. If she is innocently involved with the accident, I'd like to gain her confidence before I question her. Sam told me that Angela has signed up to go hiking tomorrow, so I was wondering if I could join you tomorrow on the hike."

"You don't need me to go on the hike. I'm sure Sam and Sarah wouldn't mind if you went hiking." Hope wasn't sure she was following his line of thinking.

"I want her to think I'm your boyfriend Hope, and of course, I don't want her to know I'm the Chief of Police. You can introduce me as a local friend of Sam's. I need to be able to move around like one of the guests for her to feel comfortable enough to talk with me."

Suddenly the hair on the back of her neck stood up—and her warning lights went on. "You're not talking about staying here, in this cabin with me are you?"

"No, not spending the night. But I would like to use your cabin as my base, so I'll need to get another key from Sarah. That's what I wanted to clear with you." He moved away from the fire and joined her on the couch. He took a sip of his wine and waited for her to respond.

"Do you really think Angela knows something?" Hope asked. She couldn't imagine how anyone could intentionally physically harm another person. She guessed that was the nurse in her—she was a healer at heart.

"I've learned long ago to follow your leads, any lead, no matter how small it may seem. And right now, this Angela person, is my only lead." He watched the fire dance from across the room and swirled his wine in the glass. He leaned back into the sofa; his eyes slowly studied the woman sitting to his side. "My only concern is that if I use this cabin, and you, as my cover, well . . . it will be very hard to "act" as your boyfriend without sharing certain intimacies with you—in public of course."

"In public? Oh, you mean like putting your arm around me or kissing me on the cheek?" Hope wasn't sure what Calder had up his sleeve, but if it would help solve the mystery of Jane Doe, she'd go along with it. And pretending to be involved with Calder wouldn't be all that difficult, but she didn't want him to know that.

"So if I say yes, when does this charade begin?"

Calder took another drink of his wine, the muscle in his jaw tightened before he spoke. "There's no time like the present, sweetheart!" he said, sounding and looking vaguely like Groucho.

Hope broke into laughter—uncontrollable laughter that brought tears to her eyes. This was the most ridiculous idea she could imagine. Here she had come to Wyoming for simplicity and to clear her head, and somehow she ended up in the middle of an attempted murder case and involved in an under cover operation! It was all so absurd!

"Now if you're going to act like that every time I call you sweetheart, I think you may blow my cover," Calder said, trying to subdue his own laughter. He began repeating the words "sweetheart" in a variety of different voices, from high pitched to imitating Clark Gable.

Her stomach ached from laughing so much. "Please. Stop," she managed to get out between laughs, holding her stomach in pain. She hadn't laughed this hard in years, and was surprised to see that Calder had tears of laughter in his eyes too. She began to wonder if she would be able to keep a straight face if he ever did call her sweetheart.

"Oh Calder, as long as you keep me laughing and keep my fire lit you can stay as long as you need." Realizing what she had just said, Hope again doubled over in laughter.

"Come on, walk me back to my truck. I'll let you have some privacy for tonight." He winked as he downed the rest of his wine and picked up his hat. "I'll be back in the morning. I think it would be good if we went to breakfast together."

"Really? Don't you think that's a bit quick—people might get the wrong idea about me," Hope wasn't sure she was ready to jump into this so fast. "Why don't you join me for breakfast tomorrow, and then we'll see what tomorrow brings." She picked up her jacket and pulled it on and she headed out to the porch.

"Whatever you say dear." He shot her a mischievous grin. "Just practicing!"

Hope gave him a playful push. This may end up being more fun than she first thought. But as they approached the truck, Hope began wondering. Would she be able to "play" along and not get involved? She was already very attracted to him; he was nice, good looking and funny. What more could a girl ask for? Yet, what was she so afraid of? Heck, she was only going to be there for two weeks; what could happen in two weeks?

Lights from inside Sam and Sarah's home provided a soft glitter to the evening as they approached the truck. Instead of opening the door, Calder leaned back against it and pulled Hope close to him. "Give me a hug like you mean it," he whispered.

She wrapped her arms around him, under his jacket and nestled her head in his chest. It was a comfort to rest against his broad shoulders and hold on to him. It felt right to be in his arms, even if it was only for looks. She better not get used to it.

Calder kissed the top of her head and wrapped his fingers in her hair, moving it away from her face. He tilted her chin up toward his, forcing her to look in his eyes. "Remember, you agreed," he said before he kissed her with a tenderness that she felt all the way down to her toes. It wasn't a hard passionate kiss, it was a tender caring kiss that lingered, a kiss that Hope recognized as the best foreplay a woman could ask for. Her reaction took her by surprise. She kept her mouth close to his, taking in his scent and sneaking soft, nibbles of kisses.

"I need to go in and get a key from Sam and Sarah," he said, breaking Hope's thoughts of fantasy. "Are you OK walking back to your cabin alone?"

"Yes Calder, it's just down the road. But it looks like folks are still in the saloon. I may just wander in and see who's there." She gave him a quick peck on the mouth. "You be careful darlin'," she quipped, gave him a wink, and sauntered away heading for the saloon. She added an extra little swing to her walk just in case he was watching. Hearing him chuckle out loud she knew that he was, but she didn't turn around; two could play this game!

In the saloon, she spotted Joe over at the game table playing a board game with some of the other kids. A few of the other guests were playing cards and Susan, John and Roger were sitting at the bar.

"Hey there, come on over the join us," John called out. "We were trying to decide if we wanted to ride tomorrow or go on the hike, or both."

Hope ordered a glass of wine from Justin, who was working the bar again. Her friends were pouring over the brochure and trail maps, trying to figure out if they wanted to ride and hike or hike the entire way. She felt lighthearted, the wine in her glass reminded her of the taste of wine on Calder's lips. She never expected to have so much fun at a dude ranch. They were laughing and joking; Hope had her arm extended across the back of Roger's chair, leaning in to get a better look at the map.

Angela entered the saloon from the side door and immediately tuned in to the laughter at the bar. Roger never looked up; never even realized she was in the same room. He seemed to be more interested in laughing with Hope and her stupid friends. She came looking for Roger to tell him that Chuck said she could go on a trail ride tomorrow. But she couldn't even get him to look up. Little miss blondie was playing up to him, teasing and tempting him. Poor Roger, women were always after him.

She stayed in the shadows, watching the group raise their glasses in a toast, and cringing every time Roger's eyes fell on Hope. Even after she had gone to great lengths to tell Hope of their wedding plans, that bitch had the nerve to sit there and flirt with him. How dare she make her look the fool!

Angela left the saloon as quietly as she entered. No one but Joe ever noticed she was there.

CHAPTER 11

HOPE TUCKED THE bottom of her jeans into heavy cotton socks and slipped on her hiking boots. She pulled the laces tight, then began the intricate weave around hooks and through loops, tightening at each level until she reached the top of the boot, wrapped the laces around her ankle and secured it with a double knot. Layering a plaid flannel shirt over a black turtleneck and t-shirt was a must for an early morning hike, and easy enough to peel off as they hiked the back ridge into the Big Horn National Forest. She glanced around the room; was there anything that she should move from view if Calder came over later? She stuck her head in the bathroom and her bedroom—nothing other than flannel pjs hanging on a hook, her toothbrush, berry body cream, and some makeup on the dresser in her bedroom. He could deal with that, after all, she had already told him about the flannel pjs. She wondered how they ever got on that conversation to begin with as she twisted her hair into a braid, and headed outside to the dining hall.

Her friend the bloodhound joined her again—she seemed to escort everyone to eat. That was her job. Then she'd sleep in the sun and hope for some treats from those she had escorted. She had such a sad face, but her tail contradicted the wrinkles and sad eyes, it wagged all the way up the hill, and with each word out of Hope's mouth it wagged faster.

John and Susan had saved her a seat and had already ordered. Pancakes for everyone—John decided they needed the carbs for their hike. The coffee was hot, with a hint of hazelnut, and Hope was ready for her second cup when she noticed Calder and Jake walking up the road. He must have parked at Sam and Sarah's.

"You remember that tall cowboy I was talking to at the Welcome party?" she asked Susan, realizing she had forgotten to set the stage for Calder's arrival. "Well I ran into him in town the other day and well, we kind of hit it off." Hope smiled into her cup and watched Susan's face. Was she going to buy her sudden confession?

Calder opened the door to the dining hall, his tall frame highlighted by shafts of sunlight.

Susan glanced at the door and then at Hope. "I'm glad you took my advice," she said, smiling as slow sly smile. "I thought he had that look in his eye." She winked at Hope as Calder removed his hat and made his way across the big room.

"Morning!" he said as he approached the table. He reached down and planted a kiss on Hope's cheek.

"Susan. John. This is my friend Calder Elliott," Hope said and continued referring to Calder as a friend of Sam and Sarah's that she had met on her flight from Salt Lake, avoiding any mention of him being Buffalo's Chief of Police. Sam had already spoken with the staff to keep Calder's occupation a secret—saying that he didn't want the guests to be concerned or feel as though they were being watched. As far as the staff or guests knew, Calder was there because of his interest in Hope.

Hope sat back and relaxed as Calder quickly engaged John and Susan in conversation. She watched his nuances, the way he handled his coffee cup, the attentive way he listened, and the fact his shirt was ironed. Most guys going hiking wouldn't go to the trouble of ironing a shirt. But that was Calder. His look was rugged, but not sloppy. He smelled clean, like soap and shaving cream and she felt proud to be sitting next to him, even though their connection was just a cover. As much as she didn't want to admit it, she was enjoying the moment.

His skin had a healthy tan, and against his dark hair it seemed to glisten. His scar was faint, and disappeared into his smile time and time again. She was concentrating on him when she heard Susan say, "What about you Hope, have you ever spent any time in the Keys?"

She felt a flush of color on her cheeks. Had she been caught ogling Calder? "No, but that is one place I would love to visit. From everything I've heard and brochures I've seen, it's very appealing," she added, hoping no one realized her attention was on Calder and not the conversation.

"Well, if you ever decide to go, please call us. We have a condo in the Keys and you are more than welcome to join us or use it when we're not there." John said, glancing back and forth between Hope and Calder, extending the offer to them as a *couple*.

"That's a real generous offer," Calder replied. "We might just take you up on that sometime, right Hope?" Calder turned sideways and put his hand on Hope's shoulder, rubbing it slowly. His touch sent a shot of warmth through her body.

"I think it would be great fun, and you could direct us to all the hot spots." Hope said going along with the idea, yet slightly concerned that Calder was ready to pull out a calendar and schedule a weekend in the Keys for them—as a couple! How far was he planning on taking this cover?

The group lingered over breakfast, laughing and discussing everything from deep-sea to fly-fishing, from travel to cooking. Hope was amazed at Calder's ability to connect with strangers and wondered if he had always been that way or if that was something he learned at the FBI. After all, he had been taught by the pros. But his interest in John and Susan wasn't phony, it was a genuine interest—and was one more thing to add to his charm.

With forty-five minutes to kill before meeting up with the hiking group, they decided to go back to the cabin. Hope was nervous. It was starting; he was going to be in her space. This wasn't like yesterday when she knew he would leave after a few minutes; now he was going to be around constantly. But at least he didn't expect to sleep at her place. Yes, he would have to leave at night, she didn't want to take any chances of sitting around drinking wine and one thing leading to another. It would be hard enough as it was not to let the charade get out of hand—she enjoyed his company but was determined not to fall for the cowboy cop.

On the porch, the dogs showed their excitement at the biscuits that Hope brought out for them. Jake fell into place walking on Calder's left, Hope was on his right. Reba, the bloodhound, stayed on the porch waiting for more treats.

"You have nice friends," he said, reaching for her hand and giving it a squeeze.

"They are nice, and a lot of fun. And it's obvious they are happy to be together. That's something I don't see often enough." Hope thought of her friends in Charlotte. So often she thought they were competing against each other, trying to out-do the other with entertainment or show. Their attempts to impress each other seemed more important than taking time to know if they really liked each other as friends. Who knew? Maybe John and Susan acted the same way when they were home. But here, they seemed to truly enjoy each other. What was it about this lifestyle that seemed to bring out the good in everyone? Maybe it was just the fact that for once, all any of them had to do was relax and have fun. How often did that happen in the real world?

Jake's nails clicked on the wood as they climbed the steps to the cabin. He found a sunny spot on the deck and curled up for a morning nap, keeping one eye on the cabin door. Calder and Hope went inside.

"I checked the sign-up list for the hike, and Joe, Roger, and Angela are on it. I'm not sure who signed up when, but their names were in order. Her name was last."

"That should be interesting. I had the idea that Roger was trying to keep Joe and Angela apart, but who knows."

"If I fall back or complain of a blister or sore foot, don't worry about me and just keep on going."

"Now wouldn't that look kind of funny? You and me supposed to be an item and I just walk on and leave you? I don't think so Calder. I wouldn't treat my worst enemy that way!" Hope added, not wanting him to think that her concern would have anything to do with her feelings.

"Well then I'll have to make sure I don't play it up too much—thanks for the warning!"

"Listen Calder, I've been thinking, and I don't know why I even mentioned Angela to you. There's no way she could be connected to the accident. She might be a bit obsessed with Roger, but surely that doesn't make her a murderer. I'm sure there are plenty other red-heads in Buffalo that wear make-up."

"No one is accusing her of murder. Remember, Jane Doe is still alive. I just want to talk to her without sending up any red flags." He looked at her for a moment, uncertain of her change of mind. Was she having second thoughts about being involved in his cover, or did she really believe that Angela was not the person in the hospital? After all, Hope had met Angela, and he hadn't. But this was his first lead and he had to check it out. He needed to meet Angela, talk with her, and at least find out whether she was the woman in the hospital visiting Jane Doe.

"Well, then maybe I'll be able to confirm your feelings after the hike." Calder walked over to the window and peered out. "The hikers are starting to gather, but I don't see any redheads yet."

Hope joined him at the window, looking out across the ranch down toward the corral. Beautiful blue skies framed the rough contours of the ranch and surrounding mountains. "It's funny, I find it difficult to focus on anything but the natural beauty and magnificence of nature every time I look out the window. It's just so overpowering." She turned and looked up at Calder, his face suddenly serious. A muscle in his jaw flexed as his eyes met hers. His light scent of soap was inviting her to taste his lips as she had the night before—that lingering soft kiss that promised tenderness and passion. She tilted her head back—their lips inches apart. She could feel his breath on her skin, but the muscle in his jaw remained tight and he didn't move.

"It's the most perfect picture. That's why I live here. I lived in Chicago for several years. But that was long ago, a different lifetime. I wore a suit and tie every day. You wouldn't have recognized me, and actually, I don't remember that person very well. That person wasn't me; it was someone trying to be what others expected me to be. I was always on edge, uptight, and didn't enjoy my own company. I expected someone or something to make me happy. It wasn't until I came back to this that I exhaled, and realized that 'happy' occurs when you're in your element—when your own energy travels at an even flow, and is not dependent on external stimulants." He remained within inches of Hope, tempted to reach down and taste her moist lips, to pull her to him and caress her body. This little blonde from the south had awakened a passion in him that had long been quiet. She was comforting, caring, and provocative; she was funny, smart, and intuitive; she was sporty, elegant, and sexy. She was a city girl. And he could never again live in the city.

"Let's get out of here," he said.

*

The hikers headed north from the ranch. Calder and Hope joined up with John and Susan. Joe and Roger were up ahead. Before they started, Joe had let everyone know he was hoping they'd come across a few wild animals on their journey—he was the only one with that wish.

Angela stepped onto her porch and quietly shut the door to her cabin as the group passed. She fell in line behind Hope and Calder.

The forest was quiet and the shafts of sunlight that coursed through the trees provided a religious experience to the hikers. The layers of grass, rocks, and limbs that made up the forest floor intrigued Hope. The dirt under her feet was black—she would have to pay dearly for that dirt back home in a bag—here it was everywhere. Nature undisturbed.

The trail they followed was a natural trail, formed by moose, deer, and other animals that traveled the forest daily. But as the wrangler leading the group indicated, those animals give wide berth to hikers. Joe didn't like hearing that.

"Hi there," Calder said to Angela. The trail widened and he fell back to walk closer to her. She wore jeans, a long sleeved t-shirt, and fur-trimmed vest. Her red hair was pulled up under a cowboy hat; Calder wondered if that was the hat she wore in the hospital, and knew it was the perfect lead in to his questions. "Great morning for a hike. These hills are their prettiest in the morning, the sun knows exactly where to shine to highlight nature's beauty."

Angela kept her eyes on the trail and kept walking, ignoring Calder's attempt at small talk.

"You look familiar to me. Do you live around here?"

"Are you kidding me? Who would want to live around here? There's nothing to do."

"I guess it depends on what you like." Calder hadn't experienced such callous bitchiness in years. Her attitude was making it difficult for him to continue being civil. But he had to. "So where are you from?"

"Atlanta." She said, not offering any more conversation.

"Well you sure do look familiar, maybe it's a movie star you look like, I'll have to figure it out."

She brightened up at the mention of looking like a celebrity. Angela took advantage of every opportunity to boost her ego—maybe she should talk to this guy after all. It might make Roger jealous, and she loved to see him jealous. When he was jealous he'd do anything for her. Anything.

"My name is Angela," she said, stopping and offering her hand to Calder. "And I don't recall seeing you around here before, did you just arrive?"

"Oh no. I'm not staying here at the ranch. I'm a friend of Sarah and Sam's and live nearby. I met up with Hope, the blonde up there, on the airplane the other day and told her I'd be out to check on her. So here I am."

"Doesn't look like she's too thrilled with the visit." Angela commented. Hope had moved ahead and was walking with Susan.

"I think she's just playing hard to get." Calder winked at Angela, trying to play up to her. After a few more steps, he stopped and turned, looking directly at Angela. "I know where I saw you. It was at the hospital in town, the other day. I remember the hat . . . and the pretty face."

Angela stopped dead in her tracks; her eyes darted up to meet Calder's steady gaze. She was visibly shaken. "What would I be doing in a hospital?" She tried to laugh as though the idea was ridiculous, but her reaction wasn't natural. She looked away from him. "Wasn't me in the hospital, but you know what they say, everyone has a twin. Must have been that movie star you think I look like."

"Whoever it was, you sure do look just like her. I was pulling in and you were coming out the front door into the parking lot." He didn't want to corner her at this point, placing her in Jane Doe's room, but he had hoped he could trick her into admitting to being there.

"No. You're mistaken. Now excuse me, but I need to catch up to my boyfriend."

Calder watched as she quickly put distance between them. Questioning her was not going to be easy. Maybe he had moved in too quick, but . . . he didn't control opportunity, he just took advantage of it.

Angela quickly moved ahead to be near Roger when the group reached a clearing, but the fact he did a double take when she appeared spoke volumes. Joe looked upset, and quickly sought out Hope.

"Can I hike with you?" he asked, he scrunched up his nose making his freckles run together and drawing attention to his missing tooth. His red hair poked out from under a backward baseball cap. Hope had to laugh at the image of the little guy standing before her.

"Of course you can hike with me, but I can't walk quite as fast as you. Is it OK if we don't lead the way?" Hope had watched Joe as Angela approached Roger and knew why he had come back to her, and she wanted to give him a reason to hang back. She caught Roger's eye and he smiled, apparently pleased that Joe was with Hope. Angela saw him smile at Hope too, and glared at them. It was obvious the growing familiarity between Roger and Hope had become a thorn in Angela's side.

"Joe, this is my friend Calder. Is it OK if he hikes with us?"

"Well . . . . I guess." The boy held his hand out to shake Calder's, and within minutes the two were acting like old friends.

The hikers continued on up through the forest to where the rocks became prevalent, making hiking more difficult. Calder reached out for Hope's hand, guiding her through the rocky trail. She was enjoying all the attention, albeit for show.

"That's my dad up there in the red shirt." Joe said to Calder, identifying every rock, fern, and tree he could along the way. "And that girl with him is Angela. She's his girlfriend, or was his girlfriend or something." He said, exaggerating the word girlfriend as though just saying it would give him kooties.

"Is she nice?" Calder inquired, hoping to get a feel for the relationship through the eyes of an innocent.

"I guess she's nice to my Dad. But she doesn't talk to me." Joe replied, wrinkling his nose as he looked up. "How tall are you?" he added, never missing a step as they wound their way through the rocky terrain. "Does it look different from up where you are?"

"Do you want to see?" Calder asked and squatted down for Joe to climb on his shoulders. Joe climbed on board and as Calder stood, Joe's eyes grew big and his grin grew wide.

"Wow. This is cool up here!" He played lookout and guided Calder up the trail, ducking limbs and generally horsing around. "I can see my Dad from up here too!"

Hope watched as Calder carefully picked his way around the rocks and boulders, all the time carrying Joe on his broad shoulders as though he weighed no more than a light backpack. Muscles tightened under his jeans with each step. Being last in line had its advantages she thought, watching as muscles moved rhythmically against the denim material.

On the clearing at the top of the ridge, Calder bent down and Joe jumped off.

"Thanks for the ride," he said, offering his little hand to Calder. "See ya."

Little Joe skipped off in the direction of his dad. It was time for a break and the hikers began rooting through their backpacks for water and snacks. Calder pulled out two bottles of water and tossed one to Hope with a wink.

She wasn't sure if the water in Wyoming just naturally tasted better than at home, or if she was extremely thirsty from the hike. Either way, she quickly downed the liter of water and watched Roger, Angela, and Joe—noticing that every time Roger spoke to Joe, Angela turned away, like she didn't want to witness any interaction between the father and son. But soon after, as soon as she thought the father and son conversation had ended, she'd touch Roger, as though reminding him she was still there. Hope also noticed that Roger never once moved in the direction of Angela, nor did he try to touch her. In fact, it was quite the opposite. Every time Angela touched him, he jerked, like a snake had bitten him.

It was sad for Hope to watch Angela being rejected. Even though Roger didn't make a fool of her in public, it was obvious by his actions that he was not interested. Why would Angela have gone to all the cost and trouble to fly out here to be with him—knowing he was coming out to spend time with his son? Hope wondered what drove a woman like Angela. What drove someone to the point of obsession? And what would it take for Angela to call it a day and go home? She felt sorry for her, and wished there was something she could do to soften the blow. She knew how demoralizing the pain of rejection could be.

Joe came running up to Calder and Hope, body slamming Hope's legs and holding on to her until he caught his breath. "You going riding this afternoon?" he inquired.

"I'm not sure Joe. I was hoping I could talk this big cowboy into taking me to town." Hope said, bending down to Joe's level. From that vantage point, looking up at Calder was like looking up at a mountain. He loomed large over both of them.

"Take me with you. Please." Joe pleaded to both Hope and Calder. He lowered his eyes and frowned. A finger beckoned Hope closer, until he whispered, "Dad told Angela she could come fishing with us, and, that's no fun. Angela can't fish!" He stated very matter-of-fact, unsure how his Dad ever thought she could. "She doesn't even talk to me. Why would I want to go fishing with her?"

"Well, at least you won't have to keep telling her to be quiet." Calder raised an eyebrow as he joked, not certain if Joe would realize he was making a joke.

"Oh I get it! Yeah. Fish don't bite around noise." He squinted his eyes and scrunched up his nose again. "But I still don't want to go fishing with her." He pushed his hands in his pockets and scowled.

"It's OK with me if it's OK with your Dad," Calder relented.

Joe raced back to his Dad. From the look on Roger's face Hope could tell that he knew Joe wanted to go with her because Angela was going with him. She watched as the handsome lawyer strode toward her.

"Are you sure you don't mind taking Joe in town with you?"

"No. He is no problem at all. And we won't be long, I just wanted to pick up a few things from the grocery, and maybe pick up a newspaper. You know, see what's going on in the real world." Her wide smile and friendly manner calmed Roger's concern.

Angela leaned against a tall pine, watching their every move. She couldn't believe that blonde would flirt so openly, while she stood just twenty feet away. But she couldn't be mad at Roger. It wasn't his fault that women were so bold. Her gaze stayed fixed on Hope, studying the way she leaned toward Roger when she spoke to him, the way her braid bounced behind her head every time she moved, and her fresh Town and Country look. Angela knew women like her, women that thought they were better than others because of their money or their name. They made her sick to her stomach and always had. Her father had left her and her mother because of some high-class blonde that worked in New York, leaving Angela at the age of eleven to take care of a mother with a drinking problem. It was during those endless years of watching her mother stumble around the house, listening to her slurred speech and self-pity that Angela vowed to never let that happen to her. She would always be aware of the tricks that women used to steal a man, especially blondes. She really hated blondes.. And now, as Angela stood watching Hope laugh and talk to Roger, she knew it was time to teach Hope a lesson.

CHAPTER 12

AFTER PICKING UP a few necessities at the market, Calder had wanted to make a stop at the police station. It was just a hunch, but he wanted to run Angela's name through the computer. He also wanted to check for any further info on the car, but with Joe along, he didn't want to risk the little guy saying anything to his dad that Angela might hear. And he also needed to stop and ask Sarah to get her camera out. He wanted a picture of Angela that he could show to Nancy at the hospital. Even though Hope was having second thoughts about Angela, he felt as though he should follow that lead to see where it took him.

Roger and Angela weighed heavy in the back of his mind. He'd never been involved with a woman like Angela, and he couldn't imagine why she would want to be with someone who obviously didn't want her. How long had the affair gone on before Roger realized it was a mistake? But most of all, Calder wondered if Roger ever really loved Angela or just loved the excitement she brought to his life. From what Hope told him, Roger felt responsible for the whole mess, and is very concerned with Angela's state of mind. Apparently she threatened suicide more than once, which would explain, to some degree, Roger's tolerance of her behavior. But still, Calder couldn't help but think that Roger's actions were giving Angela hope that the relationship could somehow continue.

"Anyone want ice cream?" Calder asked, as he turned the corner and spotted a Dairy Queen. Stopping for ice cream had always been a special treat when he would ride into town with his dad, and being with Joe reminded him of his childhood. His mother had her first bout of cancer while he was a child, and it was during her illness that the elder Mr. Elliott had started the routine of making an ice cream pit stop whenever young Calder was with him. Maybe it was his dad's way of trying to ease the terror he saw in his eyes whenever he watched his mother try to hide her pain.

Joe's eyes lit up. "Really? Can I have a chocolate cone with sprinkles on top?"

"You can have anything you want. My treat." Calder replied, winking at Hope. The whole scene made him feel like they were a family. Normally he would have shied away from anything that vaguely resembled a family outing—that would require commitment and at this point in his life, he wanted to keep it simple. No strings. But oddly enough, sharing this time together was strangely appealing.

Hope watched as Calder and Joe talked about their favorite major league teams. Joe played first base in his little league team at home and was eager to tell Calder all about it. What amazed her most was the ease in which Calder spoke to Joe. He didn't talk down to him; he talked to him like a friend, interested in everything the little one had to say. But from what she had noticed, he was like that with everyone; he had a way of making whomever he was talking to feel important and special. As much as she admired that quality in Calder, it also concerned her. It made him hard to read. Was he really interested in her, or was that just his charming nature? Or was his interest in her only related to the case? And if it was, so what? Why did that all of a sudden seem to matter? She would be leaving soon, so why was this bothering her so much? Maybe her ego was a little slighted that he hadn't pursued anything more than a tempting kiss or two. Did he find her that unappealing? She was so wrapped up in thought it took her a few minutes before she realized that chocolate ice cream was dripping onto her hand.

Calder's eyes quickly focused on Hope as she gave the cone one long lick, trying to save the melting stack from near disaster, only realizing in her haste to save the leaning tower, her nose had gotten in the way. Calder chuckled in amusement and reached across the table with a napkin to wipe the ice cream from the tip of her nose. Her eyes met his and for a moment, she was with Brian. His kindness and concern, his thoughtful gestures reminded her so of Brian. Calder was the first man in six years to stir that memory, to make her aware of a feeling of warmth and being protected and cared for. For six years she had been strong, resilient to men's charms and attempts to capture her heart. Where was her resilience now?

She turned away from Calder, from his piercing dark eyes. He confused her. She had come out here to get her life and priorities in order, and for some quiet and solitude. But her vacation had been anything but quiet. This man sitting across from her had been with her from the moment she boarded the plane in Salt Lake. Why? And why was she so afraid of being close to him—he was no different from other guys that had been in and out of her life recently, or was he? She shuddered at the thought of not being in full control of her emotions. She needed time to clear her head. The horrible wreck and Calder's belief that it was attempted murder, not to mention the little scam of being a 'couple' was wearing on her. She needed to think yet hadn't had a moment alone. After they dropped off Joe she would have to tell him, she needed some space. Hope needed some time to herself.

The ice cream must have been just what Joe needed. Soon after he climbed into the back of the black pickup he was curled up on the seat, fast asleep. Hope reached back and arranged Calder's jacket around the sleeping figure. There was something so perfect about kids when they slept—an innocence and hopefulness that had to mirror their little souls.

"Do you want kids?" Calder blurted out when she turned back around to the front seat.

"Pardon me?" She asked, completely thrown off guard by his question.

"I just wondered if you wanted kids, you know, when you get married. Do you want a family?"

"Excuse me, but I don't see that being any of your business," she said in a huff. She didn't want to talk about kids—that was too personal, too intimate. Those were her dreams, her life wishes, and to lay them out on the table for him to know, made her vulnerable, and scared her more than she wanted to admit.

She glanced over at him and noticed that he had placed a toothpick in his mouth and was playing with it. The muscles in his jaw tightened.

"What is wrong with you? Up until now everything was perfect. We had a great morning, and I actually had fun following you and Joe through the market. What are you so damn afraid of Hope?"

His words were calm, not angry as she had hoped. She turned and looked out the passenger window. Damn him, how did he always know what she was thinking? Why didn't he react like other men and run?

"I'm afraid of intimacy—at least that's what all my family says. But surely you already knew that. You've probably already called my family and my office and gotten some lengthy report on me. You use those smooth FBI skills to find out everything, don't you Calder? Well just what pushes your buttons, huh? Who's the redhead in the picture in your office? Why are you so closed mouth about your past—and why did you leave the FBI to move back here, the middle of nowhere?" She was tired, angry and hurt, and her emotions drove each word, spilling out of her without control.

She needed to know who this man was that sat next to her, tugging at her heartstrings. How did he so easily break through her barrier, that wall of protection she so carefully constructed around her heart after Brian's death?

He didn't answer her questions, not about the redhead or the FBI. But maybe she found out how to push one of his buttons—his knuckles were white on the steering wheel, and the muscle in his cheek remained taut. She watched him glance in the mirror to check on Joe, but he didn't look her way. The toothpick rolled back and forth in his mouth.

"I don't think now is the time or place to have this discussion."

They drove back to the ranch in silence.

*

Calder drove directly to Roger's cabin. Hope gathered Joe's cowboy hat and bag of gummie-bears he had bought in town as Calder lifted him from the back seat. The little guy was still sound asleep.

"Thanks for spending time with him," Roger said to Hope as he used his foot to prop open the cabin door. "He really likes you and Calder and what with Angela being here . . . well, I'm just glad you didn't mind his tagging along. He really doesn't like Angela." Roger kept thanking them and apologizing for the "situation" as they walked out onto the porch.

"He was no problem, really. We enjoyed his company," she said, glancing at Calder to see if he was still angry. His face had softened but she was sure it was because of Joe, not her.

"When is it that your wife is coming?" Hope asked.

"She had said Friday, but I haven't been able to reach her on the phone. My biggest fear is that if I can't get Angela out of here, Judy will blow her stack."

"Can't say I blame her." Calder added. "I don't mean to interfere with your personal business Roger, but have you just come out and told Angela to leave? I can't imagine anyone in their right mind wanting to hang around where they weren't wanted." He said, shooting a sideward glance toward Hope. He wasn't sure if she would ever open up to him now, after the way he had clammed up on the way home. Maybe he had overstepped his boundary by getting her involved in his cover-up. And maybe, if he opened up a little, she would too. They were both pretty hard headed.

"I have *told* her. I have *asked* her. I don't know what else to do." Roger shook his head slowly back and forth, disillusioned. "She's nuts! She really is. And I certainly don't want Joe to witness any of her antics, if you know what I mean. So I don't know what else to do." He rubbed his hand over his face and looked off into the distance as though the mountains could answer his questions.

Hope had thought the mountains could answer her questions too. But so far, they hadn't.

"You know all you have to do is give the word to Sam and Sarah and they can have her escorted off the property; they don't put up with foolishness around here and will be glad to help you out," Calder said, hoping that Roger wouldn't let the situation get any more out of control.

"Thanks. I'm using that as my last resort. Right now I'm hoping and praying my persistence will convince her that it is over, and the fact that I am trying to steer clear of her, will sink in," Roger said with a sigh.

"Well, I'm planning on going on the overnight ride, tomorrow. So if you and Joe are up to it, I'll be there." Hope shot a grin of encouragement at Roger. "It will all work out Roger. I know it will. It has to—he's such a great kid." Her eyes met Calder's; his face was calmer, and she knew that now he knew the answer to his earlier question. She adored kids, and couldn't picture a family without them. But what she couldn't picture was the man who would be the father in her family picture.

They stepped off the porch and said their good-byes to Roger. As Calder approached the passenger side of the truck to open the door for Hope, she placed her hand on his. "That's OK, I'll walk from here. I need some fresh air," she said, shielding her eyes from the sun and the look of hurt now etched in his face.

"I've got to talk with Sam and Sarah, so I'll see you later." He sounded apologetic, almost injured.

Hope reached into the back of the truck and scratched Jake on the side of his face. His heavy black tail pounded on the side of the crate. "You watch out for him, OK Jake?" she whispered to the big dog as Calder got into the truck and drove off.

CHAPTER 13

SUBTLE SHADES OF pink and blue coursed across the sky like paints on a canvas as the Wyoming sun lowered over the meadows and mountains. The temperature was warmer than usual for this time of night—possibly another storm was brewing across the ridge. Calder had intentionally stayed with Sam beyond the dinner hour, not wanting to intrude on Hope's time. After all, it was her vacation. Who was he to think he could just snap his fingers and get her to change her plans, her life, for him? Who was he to think that she cared? She had made that quite clear. She wanted nothing personal from him—business only.

Maybe that's why the past three hours had been spent with Sam, downing shots, and discussing women. Talking about Kelley, Chicago, and how everything with her seemed so right for so long. But was it? Did they share anything that was real—or had he just blended in to her life? He had moved into her circle, her city. He didn't share her passion for Chicago, but they did share a lot of passion. They spent more time in bed than anywhere else. Maybe that's why his question to Hope today was so important. He never knew if Kelly wanted children. They had never talked about it.

The moon was beginning to show its face through the twilight, inviting Calder to stretch his legs and take a walk. He enjoyed listening to the sounds of the night, to the serenading crickets and frogs and his footsteps against the sand and gravel. Jake, with his stomach full from Sarah's leftovers, decided a nap was more inviting, and settled down on his favorite porch rug.

Calder headed down by the saloon; music and laughter drifted out the windows. It sounded as though they were having fun and he wondered if Hope was in there, enjoying herself, as she should. He continued on down the road and crossing the creek he spotted someone ahead of him. Was that Hope? With night falling, it was difficult to tell. But whoever it was wasn't walking at a normal pace—it was as though the person was stopping and starting, almost creeping through the night. Strange. He didn't want Hope to think he was spying on her or following her, so he fell back and watched. The bleachers offered shelter. He hid in their shadows, while keeping his eye on the erratic movement of the person ahead of him.

A swift breeze and the heavy scent of rain sliced through the quiet of the night away from the saloons and cabins. Calder strained his eyes following the figure. The person disappeared behind the barn.

Careful not to make noise, he moved away from the bleachers to the lean-to next to the barn. A horse in the side stall jerked his head up at the sound of footsteps and watched Calder with wild eyes, uncertain if he was friend or foe. Soon realizing the movement in the dark was a friend, the horse returned back to chomping on his hay, providing cover to Calder's presence.

Remaining in the shadows, Calder moved toward the corner of the barn. A light from the tack room provided backlight to someone leaning against the rails of the far corral. It was Hope. It seemed that the night had urged her out too. She was dressed in a long denim skirt and sheer gauze blouse. He felt a bit of the voyeur standing in the shadows watching her, but knew if he spoke she would think he had followed her. He hadn't. He had been following someone else. Someone who was wearing pants and had now disappeared from sight. Oh well. It must have been one of the wranglers. And he had to admit that admiring Hope's silhouette against the corral was a very pleasant way to pass time, much more fun than following some person stumbling down the ranch road.

What was a woman like Hope doing in the mountains of Wyoming? What was it she said on the plane?—She couldn't imagine doing a 180, moving from the city to this? She was a city girl, but yet, there must be something here that called to her. Was she running from something, or to it? And according to Sam, she had won a trip for two but was here alone; why?

He really tried not to make her angry. He didn't want to fall into her trap, but whenever he was close to her she got so defensive—as though something about him frightened her. Was she really afraid of intimacy, or did she say that to keep him at arms length? And that day on the mesa—she had been crying about something. But should he be so bold as to try to find out why?

*

A nervous shiver caught Hope by surprise, causing her to turn and look over her shoulder—she felt as though someone was watching. But it was difficult to see in the night. A lone light hanging by the tack room made the rest of the area disappear in darkness. She rubbed her arms together trying to shake the uneasy feeling. It was probably just one of the wranglers in the barn.

Thunder rumbled in the distance and the smell of rain came with a rush of wind. She pulled her collar up and turned into it. The air felt cool and clean against her face. She closed her eyes to soak in the fresh feeling. It tickled her skin and seemed to clear her head, clearing away all the cobwebs that had cluttered her mind and her life since Brian's death.

It was almost too symbolic, this cleansing ritual. But it made sense. It was the reason she was here. And perhaps, it was Brian's way of saying goodbye—maybe it was his spirit in the wind that now eased her mind and opened it to life once again. It had been closed for so long.

Who was she kidding? She would have welcomed cobwebs—but no—the only thing occupying her mind and heart was emptiness. Loneliness—a feeling of not even existing.

It was that void that had driven Hope. As a real estate agent, she was driven to be the best and sell the most. But once she achieved that, she realized it wasn't what she really wanted. It wasn't enough. So she added the fast life—wild parties and a list of Mr. Wrong's to her list. Yet that feeling of nothingness remained—nothing happened, and that door to her mind, her heart, remained closed. She had slammed it shut when Brian died for fear of ever again feeling such emptiness and pain. Yet by slamming it shut she not only blocked *out* any compassion or love—she also blocked *in* any feelings of compassion or love. And only through giving could she heal.

Her biggest fear was feeling emotion, letting it touch her and wash over her. She couldn't allow that to happen, for emotions were trusting and blind to betrayal. No, she couldn't let down her guard again, especially when it came to men.

That's why Jane Doe was different. Jane Doe was an innocent—not demanding, not asking, and not giving—just there.

For the first time in years, Hope reached out to someone in truth, through her heart—not expecting anything in return. Yet the return she received had gently touched her heart and soul. It made her think—maybe she should reconsider her first love—nursing. She wouldn't make the money she made now but all that had gotten her were loneliness and empty promises.

Yes, she was at Snowy Creek for a reason.

She focused on inhaling the cool air and looked up toward the night sky that now reached out to touch her face with droplets of rain.

Lightning flashed across the sky, startling her back to reality. The raindrops grew larger, and fell faster. If she didn't want to get drenched she had better head for cover. The tack room was closest. Maybe the rain would be brief, or she could find a slicker to wear back to the cabin.

She ran to the tack room and was soon out of the rain. The room was dark and the smell of used leather and horse sweat overwhelmed the small space. But something didn't feel right. She glanced around. In the dark of the night she couldn't make out anything other than the saddles, sitting diligently on their rack under nameplates on the wall. She stood with her hand on the door, just in case she needed to make a speedy departure. Her instincts told her she was not alone.

"Hello." Her voice was nervous and soft. "Is anyone there?"

Quiet. She could feel the adrenaline pumping through her veins, her heart rate raced.

"Who's there," she asked again, this time in a firm controlled tone.

Hope heard noise from the back of the tack room. Bits and bridles jingled. The cold hand of fear shot through her bones. Before she could turn and focus on the noise, blackness appeared to her side. Pain shot through her body like lightning in the night sky and she let out a blood-curdling scream as the blunt force of a wide barn shovel slammed into her shoulder.

She stumbled out onto the porch of the tack room, under the lone light grabbing her shoulder and writhing in pain. Calder was across the paddock in an instant.

"My God! What happened?" he asked, his eyes wide with concern. "Are you OK?" Rain pelted them as he scooped her into his arms and carried her to the safety and shelter of the shed by the barn.

"Someone hit me with a shovel," she said, trying to catch her breath. "Who in the world . . . did you see anyone?"

"Stay here, and be quiet," he said, planting her against the barn. He ran back across the paddock and into the tack room. The discarded shovel lay just inside the door. The back door of the tack room stood ajar—the obvious escape route. He peered from the rear of the tack room, trying to identify where the person wielding the shovel could have gone. He thought he saw movement by the barn, moving toward the spot where he had placed Hope.

"Hope—it's OK. There's no one here," he called out from the tack room and quickly strode toward the barn, knowing the person he saw in the shadows had to know he was there. "You must have stepped on the shovel in the dark and it jumped up and hit you in the shoulder. There is no one here."

Her mouth opened wide in disbelief; he reached up and covered her mouth with his hand. Fear and questioning filled her eyes as his hand muffled her words. "Shh," he whispered. "The person after you is still in the barn."

Her adrenaline continued to pump through her with the same intensity of the pain in the shoulder she held on to. Her mind reeled with questions, had someone mistaken her for an intruder?

Lights cut through the rain and darkness, blinding Calder and Hope as a truck pulled up to the barn. Sam and Justin jumped out of the cab.

"Sorry folks, didn't mean to interrupt anything," Sam grinned sheepishly and tipped his hat toward the couple. "We just came down to make sure everything's ready for the ride tomorrow. We're packing up all the saddlebags tonight."

Calder crossed over to Sam and Justin and whispered something to them. In the blink of an eye, Calder whisked Hope into the truck and Justin jumped in the driver's seat.

"I've been instructed to get you out of here and back to your cabin." Justin remarked when he saw the confused look on Hope's face. "Calder will meet you there after they check the barn, and you're to lock your door," he said, squealing his tires as he quickly pulled away from the barn.

"What in the sam hill happened?" Justin asked.

"I think I surprised someone in the tack room." Hope was trying to piece together what had just happened. "And the next thing I knew someone walloped me with a shovel." Hope cringed as she rubbed her arm.

"Yeah, well I wish I would have surprised them. The tack room is my responsibility, and if anyone is messing with the tack I'd be pretty upset," Justin stated as he pulled to a stop in front of Hope's cabin. He followed her up the steps and insured the cabin was safe before heading back to join Calder at the barn.

Hope paced back and forth from the living room to the kitchen, peering from the windows that overlook the barn, straining her eyes to see any movement from that direction. Minutes seemed like hours, while the rain and lightning continued to assault the night.

She finally heard the comforting low rumble of Calder's truck. Jake was at Hope's door before Calder was on the stairs. She opened the door for the big black dog knowing Calder was right behind. He stepped into the cabin and into Hope's arms. Their embrace revealed a sense of urgency, a need to share feelings of relief that both were safe.

"What happened?" she asked, stepping back to look at Calder and make certain he was all right.

"We're not certain. But the person got away. Probably made a run for it when Sam and Justin pulled up. We went through the barn and the tack room. We didn't find anyone and it didn't appear that anything was missing. But someone was up to something or they wouldn't have attacked you. I'm sure it was just a matter of being in the wrong place at the wrong time." Calder tried to ease her concern, all the while knowing that the person he followed was probably the one who attacked Hope, and something about their movement made him think it was a woman.

"But that means they were doing something illegal, immoral, or indecent, doesn't it?" Hope questioned, as she paced back and forth in the small room.

"Well whatever they were up to they definitely didn't want you there," he said, raising an eyebrow.

"They?"

"Semantics. I'm sure it was only one person."

Hope stopped suddenly and turned to look at Calder. "You haven't told me what you were doing down there," Hope asked, half questioning, half accusing.

"You've got to be kidding. You don't think it was me, do you?" Calder questioned with a puzzled look on his face.

"No. But what . . . I don't know what to think anymore. Were you following me?" Hope was confused, her get away from it all vacation had turned into a nightmare; she didn't know what to believe.

"I wanted to talk to you but didn't know what to say—so I went for a walk. I thought it would clear my head. Halfway down the road I thought I saw someone walking toward the barn. But by the time I got down there the person I was following went into the barn. At the same time I saw you over at the corral."

"I was communing with nature."

"Well, you were deep in thought and didn't look like you wanted two-legged company. So I didn't say anything to you. By then I figured the person I followed was one of the wranglers. Sam and Justin say not."

"I guess I surprised him when I ran in to the tack room to escape the rain. He wasn't expecting company."

"Did you see anything? Can you remember anything at all that might tell if it was a man or woman who attacked you?"

"No. It happened so fast, all I remember is seeing a shadow, and then feeling an intense burning pain in my shoulder. I don't know if it was a man, woman, tall, short. I don't know."

"But you were standing out in the middle of the paddock. If I saw you then the other person did too." Calder hesitated for a moment before continuing, "I don't think you surprised anyone Hope. I believe that person followed you."

"But that doesn't make any sense. Who would follow me, and why? If it was a guest or wrangler, I'm sure they would have called out to me. Said something." Hope dismissed the notion that anyone intentionally followed her. "I'm sure whoever it was went down to check on something and I probably scared the heck out of them when I entered the tack room."

Calder crossed the room to be near her by the window. He reached down and laced his fingers in her damp curls. "I just want you to be careful. Jane Doe is a case of attempted murder. And now you're in jeopardy. I never should have compromised your safety. I've involved you in something I shouldn't have."

He stood close, his hand continuing to stroke her hair. The tension of the day had built to a crescendo. She could feel her pulse race and a need to be held by him again. He was honest with his words, would his emotions be honest too? Were hers?

She turned away from the window and into his arms. Her eyes caught his and without saying a word, their lips met. This time it wasn't a show for others, or because she had been crying. This time it was from a deep need, a private personal desire that now roared inside her. His kiss was tender and hesitant, as though he was asking for permission. She answered with a passion she didn't know was in her. Her arms wrapped around his broad shoulders, running her fingers through his dark curly hair, still wet from the rain. The smell of soap mixed with sweat and rain attacked her senses with a rush of passion. It was a sweet clean scent that she had come to identify with him.

"There's something I need to know," she asked, biting at her bottom lip.

"Anything for another kiss," Calder replied, his dark eyes twinkling with delight.

"The brunette who picked you up at the airport. Do you date her?"

"Date? Well, you could call it that—I see her about once a month," Calder confessed. "She's my sister, Colleen." He chuckled, knowing he had Hope wondering for a minute. "She goes to school down in Denver and comes up here to visit me and Dad when she's got time."

"Sister, huh?" she asked, questioning whether or not she should believe him.

"Cross my heart," he said, using his index finger to cross his heart, then reached toward Hope and traced along her cheek with the same finger. He moved his finger down to her mouth, and outlined it, rubbing gently against soft, pouty lips. His finger then pulled her in to his welcoming kiss.

He reached behind her and switched off the cabin lights. The flames of the fire danced in the dark, enhancing their growing desire. The cracking and popping of the kindling combined with the beat of a steady rain provided erotic background music in the small space.

Calder's body pressed Hope against the wall; she could feel his longing for her. She relaxed into him as his attentions moved to her neck and chest, his tongue tracing along sensitive skin between soft kisses. Her breath quickened as his fingers deftly found white lace under her gauze shirt. His hands felt like velvet as he gently teased and aroused her. The fire within her body exploded with each kiss, each revealing touch. Their greedy mouths connected once again, revealing new needs, and ravenous passion.

He stopped and pulled away from her; his eyes questioned their actions.

"Don't you dare stop now," she purred.

"Your arm—is it OK?" he asked, his voice soft, his finger slowly tracing around the area that would soon turn black and blue.

"What arm?" she replied with a throaty chuckle, gazing into his eyes and nibbling on his bottom lip.

They moved as one to the sofa in front of the fire. She fumbled with the buttons on his shirt; it fell to the floor as she ran her hands across his chest and pressed her mouth to his warm body. She watched every move as he untied her gauze blouse and carefully eased it over her head. His mouth reached down and covered hers, and the hair on his chest felt like a feather tickling her bare skin.

The storm outside continued; rain, wind, and distant thunder provided nature's sensuous song. It was the perfect accompaniment to their raw, yielding emotion.

Shivers of delight raced through her as he pulled her close and again claimed her mouth; the sensation of his bare skin providing intense pleasure. Their hands raced to know each other, to take possession of each previously unseen or untouched part. Her eyes wandered over his sleek muscled body. He was strong and hard and with the glow of the fire behind him, his body glistened with desire.

Calder tossed a pillow and blanket on the floor in front of the fire. And in what seemed like slow motion, lowered her to the floor, his body entwined with hers, moving in rhythm with the blaze of the fire, and passion of the storm.

They made love throughout the night—their desires baring the need in their souls.

CHAPTER 14

CALDER WOKE EARLY. Embers in the fire still glistened hot orange. Hope lay next to him, curled into his body, keeping him warm against the cold; once again arousing his desire.

He slipped out of their makeshift pallet and tucked the blanket around her. She looked innocent and vulnerable lying there—not at all the fireball that aroused and responded to him again and again throughout the night. Strands of golden hair slightly hid her face—a face that had captured Calder's attention from the first moment. Her skin was lightly tanned and soft to the touch. Her lips curved upward in a natural smile. Like his mother would say, she had a clean, honest face—beautiful too.

Calder pulled on his jeans and stumbled into the kitchen, rubbing his eyes to clear the sleep from them and running his fingers through his hair to comb it. He'd need a pot of coffee to clear his mind from the night of lovemaking and to prepare for what he knew would be a long day.

He had agreed to ride with Sam and Justin, taking the packhorses and chuck wagon to the overnight spot. They planned on heading out early in order to get everything set up and ready for the ranch guests. And packhorses and wagons don't move as fast as riders. The over-night rides were always a highlight at the ranch. Tents would be set up for those who wanted some privacy, or in case of rain. So far, the weather appeared perfect.

Jake rose from his spot under the kitchen table and gave a good long stretch, his butt high in the air, front legs reaching out. He circled three times and lay back down, his eyes continued to follow Calder around the kitchen.

"Hey boy," Calder whispered, finally turning his attention to the big black dog. "Wanna go out?" he asked. No sooner were the words out of his mouth than Jake was at the door, tail wagging. They stepped onto the deck and Calder gently pulled the door shut so as not to awaken Hope. Once outside, Jake bounded down the steps onto the grass.

Calder pulled on his jacket and breathed in the cool morning air. It was perfection. Dawn. Calder loved this time of day. Shafts of morning light pointed their thin knobby fingers over the crooks and crags of the mountaintops. He watched the mountains change color, grow and expand—nature slowly awakening. It was a magnificent event. Every day. He loved Wyoming.

*

Light streamed in the windows of the little cabin. Hope tightened her robe and poured a fresh cup of coffee. She leaned against the kitchen counter to read the note one more time.

"It's early—no one will see me. My truck is down at Sam's. No one will know I was here—but you, Jake and me. Jake's sworn to secrecy, and I could never put last night into words. Later gorgeous. CE"

She grinned from ear to ear each time she read the note. Remembering the intensity of the night brought a flush to her cheeks. She had never expected the evening to end up that way, but thinking back, it made sense. Her nerves were raw, exposed after the assault in the tack room, and his sensuality and concern hit her like one of the lightning bolts in the storm. Their need to be understood exploded with passion. As though they had finally found a common language.

Hope studied his writing; it was printed in all capitals, and not at all difficult to read. Scrawling, but structured. Rather like him.

She wondered why he didn't wake her before he left, but maybe it was best he hadn't. If he had he may well still be here. Then everyone would know he spent the night, and even though they were supposed to be a couple, Hope was concerned about Sam, Sarah, and Justin. They knew the truth.

The fire crackled and fell into a pile of radiant embers. The log Calder had put on before he left had finished. Perfect timing. It seemed that everything Calder did was perfectly timed. Why in the world was he a cop?

His keys lay next to the note and she remembered their middle of the night conversation about Jane Doe. Since the overnight trail ride didn't begin until 1:00 PM, she had plenty of time to take his truck in to town and check on their patient. As of yesterday, there was still no change. She wanted to check the newspapers too. By now, someone had to have reported her missing. At a time like this, she wished she had a way to check her laptop. Perhaps there was a computer at the library she could log on to. Yes, she'd stop by the hospital first, and then the library.

Hope had quickly gotten accustomed to dressing in layers. The morning and night always brought a brisk chill, while the warmth of midday mountain sunshine was more like the temperatures of home. This morning, she added another t-shirt layer. It seemed cooler than usual. Perhaps she was just remembering the heat of the night.

Susan and John waved as she entered the dining hall. She didn't have time for a big breakfast, or to chitchat, but wanted to see if her friends were going on the overnight ride.

"You ready?" she asked, her eyes widened in excitement as she slid in the seat across from Susan.

"Obviously not as ready as you! Look at you—you're beaming!" Susan eyed her friend and slowly smiled. She knew the look. "I don't think all this enthusiasm is over a trail ride. A ride maybe, but not on a horse!"

"Susan!" Hope replied, blushing with embarrassment over being so transparent.

A cup of coffee and menu appeared before her and she warmed her hands on the steaming mug. If Susan were by herself, she'd be tempted to tell her about Calder, but she wasn't so she wouldn't. Hope knew she couldn't fool her new friend, but also knew she needed to change the subject. She also decided not to say anything about the shovel incident. "Just toast this morning please," she told the young wrangler waiting on her.

"I'm not going out with the day group—I'm going on the afternoon ride, and we don't leave until one. This morning I'm going in to town. Hopefully there's a computer in the library I can log on to. I've got to check on some things from work," she added, hoping she sounded believable. But saying that made her realize that sooner than she wanted, she would be going back to work, back to e-mails and phone calls and no time for herself. It was funny, she hadn't realized just how much she had relaxed and adapted to life without technology since she arrived. Putting on a suit and heels hurt to think about it.

Her friends from home probably wouldn't recognize her—and will find it hard to believe how perfect this vacation was. Even though Calder had woven his way into every day of her vacation, it wasn't just him that was making it special. She had to admit he was charming and yes, the passion they shared last night was nothing short of perfect. But she had a feeling of being at home out here. Everything here felt right.

"John's decided not to go on the overnight. There's a rodeo in Sheridan tonight he wants to go to, you know, experience some local color."

"Me and saddles don't get along too good after an hour or so." John said as he wriggled around in his chair.

"Yes and I'm still sore from the other day," Susan added "but I really want to go on the overnight. So I'm still trying to decide if I want to go without John on the overnight or join him for the rodeo."

"Well the afternoon ride doesn't leave until one o'clock, so you have some time to decide."

"Are you taking a change of clothes or anything to sleep in?" Susan asked, unsure of what to expect.

But Hope was distracted and didn't answer. Angela was standing at the door looking around the dining room. She scanned each table, and stopped when she saw Hope. Daggers leaped from her eyes as she cross the room.

"Hope, did you . . . ," Susan asked, interrupted halfway through her sentence by the sudden appearance of Angela.

"Listen Blondie," Angela hissed. "You need to mind your own business and leave Roger and his son alone. Joe is just playing games. His mother has done everything possible to make him hate me. But I'm going to make this work. I'm going to marry Roger, and no one is going to change that. Understand?" Angela stood by the table, one hand on her hip. Her nostrils flared as her voice got louder. The noisy dining hall became suddenly quiet.

Hope watched, shocked by the sudden intrusion on her perfect morning. The whole scene was like something from a movie.

"What are you talking about?" Hope finally muttered, confused as to why Angela thought she was after Roger.

"You know damn well what I'm talking about," she leaned on the table and got within inches of Hope's face. "Stay away from Roger and Joe!" she threatened, then turned and marched out of the dining hall.

The noise level returned to normal after the door slammed behind her.

"I hope it hit her in the butt!" Hope said as she quickly analyzed what had just happened.

"Whoa—what was that all about?" Susan asked whoever was listening. "Man that girl has a screw loose."

"Definite loose cannon—that one." John added.

"She is weird, but I almost feel like I should talk to her. She's got it all wrong if she thinks I'm after Roger, and she needs to know that."

"You need to do no such thing," Susan stated firmly. "If anything—you need to stay as far away from that nut case as possible. Trust me Hope—she's a lost cause."

"If I were Roger I'd be worried," John said. "She's a real fatal attraction."

"Well, if nothing else, she gave everyone something to talk about!" Hope laughed, wanting to change the subject. She didn't want to talk about it—yet she couldn't shake the heavy feeling of déjà vu. She searched her memory trying to recover any relationships she had been in lately where a jealous ex would have approached her; but she couldn't. The heaviness remained.

After losing her appetite and forcing down the toast and coffee, Hope left her friends to finish their breakfast. The fresh air and sunshine outside helped her shake the discomfort she felt after the encounter with Angela. She had too much to do before the ride to worry about it. Reba the bloodhound raised her head as Hope walked by, but was so accustomed to her that she didn't even get up.

With Calder's keys in hand, Hope climbed into the big pickup. She had never driven a truck before but figured it couldn't be too hard to handle, and with a sore shoulder, she was glad it was automatic. She was adjusting the mirror and seat when Sarah approached, purse in hand.

"Good morning. How are you feeling this morning?" Sarah asked; giving her guest the once over to make certain she was all right.

"It's starting to bruise a bit, but other than that I'm fine," Hope said. "Really, I'm fine."

"Sam is really upset about last night. We can't imagine who would have done such a thing, or why." Sarah shook her head in dismay. "So, where are you off to so early?"

"Heading into town to the library, and the hospital to check on the patient," replied Hope.

"I was on my way in town too; I've got to go to the bank and pick up a few items at the store."

"Do you want to ride with me? That is if you trust my driving," Hope chuckled.

"If Calder gave you the keys, that's good enough for me." Sarah hiked her skirt and climbed into the truck. Country music blared from the radio as Hope cranked the engine.

"He does like his country," Sarah said with grin. Hope adjusted the volume and maneuvered the big truck back from the house, across the creek and away from the ranch. It wasn't long before Hope was at ease behind the wheel.

"Looks like someone is up early making calls too." Sarah said, nodding her head in the direction of the center of the mesa. As they got closer, Hope noticed Roger standing in the center of the mesa on a cell phone. She wondered if he was talking to his wife or work—or some other girlfriend. In her mind she still wasn't sure whom to believe, or, just how much of Roger's story was true and how much of Angela's was true. The way things were going, she had a feeling it was a little of both.

"I heard about what happened at breakfast, and I have to apologize. That was uncalled for." Sarah shifted in her seat, leaning against the door, her gaze steady on Hope. "You don't think she was the one with the shovel do you? If so, we are going to have to get her off our property."

"No. Certainly not—I would think if she was behind the shovel, she wouldn't have been so quick to threaten me in public." Hope had already considered that possibility after the breakfast incident, but quickly dismissed it.

"Well, you're probably right. But still . . . I'd be leery of that woman." Sarah cleared her throat and continued. "After talking with Calder last night, Sam and I have decided we have to do something to compensate you—your "free" vacation is turning out to be anything but a vacation. Like Calder said, you haven't had a chance to really enjoy yourself, he's had you so wrapped up in the hit and run—and now you being attacked, it's just horrible. Would you like to stay another week—or perhaps plan a return next year, on us?"

"Oh Sarah, that is so kind of you, but really, Jane Doe is certainly not your fault; nor was last night. I must say, it's not quite the vacation I had in mind when I left home last week." She chuckled thinking about how much had happened in such a short time. "But it will definitely be one I'll remember," she said; and meant it.

"Well there's got to be something we can do that you will accept. So think about it. I won't let you leave here until we make a deal." Sarah's generosity was real and Hope knew from the tone of her voice she meant it. She had experienced more openness and caring since arriving in Wyoming than ever before. She remembered what Calder said on the plane about living here. The people say what they mean and mean what they say. He was right. Again.

"There is one thing," Hope said, keeping her fingers crossed that she wasn't stepping over the line with what she was about to ask. "You've known Calder for a long time and I was wondering . . . I know he was with the FBI, I saw the pictures in his office, but he didn't want to talk about it. It obviously meant a great deal to him or he wouldn't have those reminders around him. What happened? Why did he leave such a promising career?"

Hope glanced over at Sarah who sat still, eyes straight ahead. Her face was serene, unreadable, and it seemed like forever before Sarah spoke.

"I know Calder cares a great deal for you Hope. And because of that, I think you should know. Ever since Calder was a kid, he wanted to be in the FBI. Kids in the city dream of the wide-open west, and kids in the west dream of the city. Go figure. So after college he applied to the academy. He was accepted, and for the first time in his life he left the mountains of the west. He moved to New York first. He loved his job but hated the city. No trees, no hawks, and to hear Calder tell it, nothing real. Anyway, he transferred out of New York to Chicago, a little closer to home. It was there he met Shelley. He described her as having hair the color of autumn and looking as Irish as a four-leaf clover. He was a man in love and it didn't take long before he asked her to marry him. But Shelley was a city girl, with city friends. And Calder never quite fit in. She worked in an art gallery and her friends, well, they lived a life style that Calder didn't approve of or understand. Apparently he tried to persuade Shelley that her friends' avant-garde lifestyle could be bordering on illegal, but Shelley remained committed to her friends. One night after a bitter disagreement, Shelley took off with her friends. There was a terrible accident and everyone died on impact, except Shelley. And she blamed Calder. His world fell apart that night. He couldn't believe she really *blamed* him for the wreck. But she did, and she ended their engagement that night. His disdain for the city returned with a vengeance. He blamed *it* for the wreck and for Shelley leaving him. Not long after, his mom went into terminal stages of cancer, and he returned home for good."

They had driven all the way in to town by the time Sarah finished her story. Hope pulled up in front of the bank and turned off the motor. She sat in silence for a few moments trying to make sense of her emotions. Part of her wanted to cry and part of her felt as though she had just trespassed on sacred ground. And part of her realized that Sarah had just shared a secret with a friend.

"Thank you." Hope said, reaching across the truck to hug Sarah. "That explains a lot."

"I didn't tell you anything that he wouldn't tell you sooner or later. But sometimes later can be too late." Sarah opened the door to the truck and added, "Take your time Hope; don't rush on my account. I'll be in the park across the street whenever you're ready to head back."

Hope watched from the truck as Sarah entered the bank, speaking to everyone she passed and wondered what it would be like to live in a town where you knew practically everyone.

*

The vision of Shelley from the picture in Calder's office and the story of their romance filled her head as she turned the black truck into the police station parking lot. She wanted to go back in his office and take another look at the woman who had broken his heart, but decided against it. Someone might find her snooping.

Doris was on the dispatch radio but motioned for Hope to come closer. She handed her a slip of paper while continuing to talk and take instruction from the radio.

"B.Y. Rentals—Judy Longacre—Atlanta, GA." Hope read the scrawling writing but was unsure what it meant. The name Longacre sounded vaguely familiar.

"Ten-four," Doris signed off and turned her attention to Hope. "Well, Calder was right. B.Y is a new rental car company. All the way down in Salt Lake. I can't tell you the hours I've spent calling every car rental company between here and Denver—and nothing. But Calder insisted. Find out if there are any new rental companies—those not listed in the phone book, he kept saying. And sure enough, wouldn't you know. Bingo. There's a match on the VIN number. That smashed up car belongs to B.Y. Rentals in Salt Lake, and Jane Doe now has a name."

Hope thought Doris would never get done talking. Her heart raced as she realized how important this was, and Calder was in the mountains, in the middle of nowhere, riding with a wagon and pack horses; there was no way to reach him.

"Have you contacted her family?" Hope asked.

"I've been trying. So far no luck." Doris ruffled through the papers on her desk and picked up another scrap of paper. It seemed there was no order on Doris' desk, and everything was on torn bits of paper. "Here it is . . . I have an address in Atlanta. I've contacted the Atlanta PD—they will continue to try to get in touch with the family. So far, no luck."

"Calder will be thrilled, I just wish there was a way we could contact him, or you could contact him if you get any more information." Hope recognized the look of ownership on Doris' face and didn't want her to think she was claiming any responsibility for Doris' hard work.

"One more thing. If you're going to see Calder before I do, let him know his friends in Chicago haven't been able to match the prints he sent off." Doris was all business, and wanted to make certain that Calder knew that even though they had a name for Jane Doe, she was pursuing the case.

"What prints? He didn't say anything about lifting any prints," Hope wondered.

"Nothing personal, but I'm sure there's a lot more going on in that head of his than he'd ever share with a woman. If you know what I mean," Doris stated in a matter-of-fact tone.

Yes. Hope should have known better than to think that Calder had confided all he knew about the case to her. Brian never had. Brian would never talk about work. Period. Not the people he worked with, his cases. Nothing. He didn't want to worry her. Little did he know that *not* telling her was worse. Her imagination ran rampant. And the day he was shot, she felt like a stranger around his friends. She couldn't even grieve with them; they knew a different man.

She thanked Doris for the information and headed out of the police station, anxious to get to the hospital and the library—and unsure of where to go first. A trip to the library might reveal a story regarding a missing person named Judy Longacre from Atlanta—and this may shed some light on who was responsible for the attempt on her life.

It amazed her how responsible she felt for Jane Doe—or Judy. And it seemed strange to call her by another name. Hope had come to think of Jane Doe with affection and concern, and affection and concern were feelings that had been foreign to her for quite some time. Tears clouded her vision and she swallowed hard to regain control of her emotions after realizing that she may be the first person since the accident to call her by name. Without hesitation, she headed in the direction of hospital.

Nancy, the head nurse, was on duty when Hope arrived. Her eyes danced when she looked up at Hope over reading glasses.

"Good morning . . . here to see our patient?" Nancy asked.

"Yes. And I have wonderful news!" Hope grinned from ear to ear with excitement. "It appears that Jane Doe's real name is Judy Longacre," she announced. "I can't wait to see if she responds to her name—has there been any change?"

"Her vitals have rapidly improved and stabilized. If it wasn't for her comatose state, she'd be off the critical list."

Nancy picked up the chart and flipped through it. "Come on. It's time to check on her. I'll go in with you and monitor her when you speak her name. This may be the breakthrough she needs."

Hope followed Nancy into Judy's room, remaining at the door while Nancy did a quick check of the monitors and many tubes that led in and out of Judy's body. She knew the procedure well. It was second nature to her yet she hadn't really thought of her nursing career since she had left it, years before. But somehow, here on the ward, it was as though a warm childhood memory had invaded her senses. A sense of euphoria from being reunited with a loved one washed over her; she had a strange desire to pick up Judy's chart just to feel the cool metal, to see if it would again be a good fit in her hands.

"Go ahead." Nancy whispered. "Call her name."

"Hey there." Hope wanted to connect with whatever senses were receptive; hoping to arouse them from their deep sleep. She stroked Judy's hair to let her know someone was with her, someone who cared. "You're really doing well—improving everyday. I'm so proud of you." She held on to her hand. Her mouth was within inches of her ear. "Judy?" she asked. She looked up at Nancy for any indication. Nancy didn't smile—she slowly shook her head from side to side.

"Judy? Judy Longacre?" Hope tried again; but still no response. What if Jane Doe wasn't Judy Longacre? What if she had used someone else's license? No. This was the first real lead and she wouldn't allow that thought to enter her mind.

"Don't be discouraged. Now that we have a name you can be certain we'll use it every time we walk into the room." Nancy's reassurance was well received. Hope knew better than to expect a miraculous awakening just from hearing her name, but it had happened before. She had heard about cases where a relative's voice, the presence of a beloved pet, or that certain music had played a vital part in bringing patients out of a coma.

She looked down at the small figure lying in the hospital bed. Her face was still loaded with stitches, but the swelling had gone down. Tubes and machines were attached everywhere, recording every move, every breath.

"Calder said you used to be a nurse," Nancy said, as she finished writing an up date in the chart. "I can see that. You have that way about you. If you don't mind me being a bit nosy, why'd you leave?" she asked. She was blunt and got straight to the point; no beating around the bush for Nancy. Hope admired that straightforwardness.

"That's a tough question. I loved nursing, everything about it." Hope reflected on it for a moment. No one else had ever asked her that question, much less someone she barely knew. But she liked Nancy; she had connected with her from the beginning. What did she have to lose by spilling her guts; she would soon be back in Charlotte. "My fiancé was a cop, and he was killed in an undercover drug deal that went bad. It all hit me so fast; I didn't know what to do. I couldn't breathe much less think, or care for a patient. I became numb. It was like all my compassion withered and died with Brian. And without compassion, I wasn't a nurse. I wasn't doing myself or my patients any good." She stood up and ran her hand along the stainless steel bedrail. It was sleek and cool, and precise, like the exactness of nursing. While the bed linens were soft and warm, reminding her of the comfort in nursing. It was a paradigm that had always amazed and encouraged her. "I left; I ran. I ran as far away from nursing as I could and I've been running since."

"I'm sorry, Hope. I didn't mean to open an old wound." Nancy said, straightening the blanket and sheets around Judy, sensing Hope's struggle to put her feelings into words.

"You didn't. For some reason it's been on my mind ever since I got here. Maybe it was finding Judy; maybe it was just the fact that I finally admitted to myself that I wasn't real proud of me. My fiance wouldn't know me now." It felt strangely healing to verbalize the thoughts that had been running through her mind of late. "But here, by a patient's bedside, I feel like me again. It's a strange feeling, really strange."

"Well I think the you I know is pretty special. Anyone who would take time from a well earned vacation to spend time with a comatose patient they don't even know—well you're OK in my book." Nancy put her arm around Hope and gave her a hug as they walked out of the room into the nursing station.

"I wish she would regain consciousness before I leave," Hope said, half praying out loud. "If I give you my card will you call me with updates?" she turned and looked directly at Nancy. She was wearing her heart on her sleeve and knew it.

"I promise." A soft smile broke across Nancy's face. "I'll give you weekly prognosis on our Jane Doe. I promise. Now don't worry so much. Go. Have fun. You're still on vacation!"

"Yes and I'm going on an overnight ride tonight. They are setting up camp for us somewhere in the park. Just the stars, the moon, the horses, and us city slickers." Hope beamed as she spoke of her upcoming adventure. She looked forward to the long ride, and spending the night under the stars.

"And I think it's a new moon tonight. So beware!"

"Oh no—not more local legends. Justin, one of the hands at the ranch, is full of local legends. He had me scared to death the night we came across the wreck."

"No legends—news from the Farmer's Almanac. Just be careful." Nancy chuckled to herself in amusement.

"Now what?" Hope asked.

"Is Calder going on the ride?"

"Yes—he's already left with the pack team."

"Be careful," she winked, "need I say more?"

Hope felt her face flush. She had no idea what Nancy did or did not know. "I'll watch him," she said, almost embarrassed to look her in the eye for fear she would give herself away. Even the mere mention of his name brought back the passion of the night with the impact of a tidal wave, washing over her once again, reminding her of the way his hands had studied her body, how his touch set her afire with desire. She felt like a schoolgirl who had just been caught scribbling her boyfriend's name on her notebook.

The elevator door opened and Hope stepped inside, turned, and waved as Nancy once again took position in the nursing station.

CHAPTER 15

THE TRIP TO the library turned up nothing new. Newspapers in and around the Atlanta area were absent stories on a missing woman. Hope found it hard to understand how an obviously upscale, cared-for woman could be in an accident and lie in a coma for a week with no one searching for her. It tore at her heart; was Judy that much of a loner?

But the thought that really nagged at her was wondering what if that had been her lying there in a coma instead of Judy. No one would be looking for her. A few of the girls in the office, her mother and brother were the only ones who knew where she was—but they also knew not to expect to hear from her for a couple of weeks, and a lot can happen in a couple of weeks. Could that be the case with Judy? Perhaps her friends and family weren't expecting to hear from her for several weeks. That would explain the absence of a missing person report.

Hope picked up Sarah at the park and talked nonstop on the drive back to the ranch. The news of Jane Doe now having a name was a huge break in the case. She couldn't wait to tell Calder.

"Are you sure there is no way to contact him?" Hope asked again, thinking that perhaps there was some secret means of communication that the Porter's didn't want the guests to know about.

"Short of smoke signals?" Sarah laughed at Hope's persistence. "That's why they call it getting away from it all—you are. Of course when we travel away from the ranch like that, there are some must haves—like a first aid kit, plenty of food and water, and a gun, just in case." She winked at the mention of the gun.

"I have a feeling that Calder will want to head back as soon as he hears the news about Judy. How long does it take to ride out to the camp site?" Hope was trying to calculate if they would have time to ride back to the ranch before nightfall.

"It's a hard three hour ride—usually takes twice as long for the guests. That's why we overnight, that along with the campfire songs and the great food. Nothing like a steak cooked over an open fire after riding all day."

"Hope, you need to let go of the case for now. Calder will find out soon enough and, like you said, it's not as though someone is searching frantically for your Jane Doe. Another day will not make or break the case."

"You're right. But I'm just so excited that we finally know who she is. I guess I want the case to be resolved and Judy to regain consciousness before I go home; but chances of that happening are slim to none." Hope was disappointed that reality would probably not allow things to unfold as she wanted them to. She knew that these things take time; maybe that's why she was trying to rush getting the news to Calder. Would half a day really make that much of a difference?

"I can't believe I've been here over a week, it's going by so fast," Hope added.

"Well, like I said, we could extend your stay if you can—I have an empty cabin. Would you accept that?" asked Sarah.

"I'd say you have yourself a deal! But don't expect me to sit back and relax. As long as I'm out here I plan on being as involved in this case as Calder will allow." Hope said, pulling in to the ranch.

"Knowing Calder, I'm sure he will need your undivided attention," Sarah teased.

*

The dining hall was deserted when she walked in for lunch, and for the first time since last night, she felt uneasy. She rubbed her shoulder at the thought of the shovel slamming into her. If she had happened upon one of the wranglers in the tack room, Hope wouldn't have known if they were supposed to be there or not, so why would they want to harm her? Or maybe they thought she was a thief. Looking at the lunch menu she decided she'd probably never know who hit her or why. She was just in the wrong place at the wrong time.

After a quick bowl of soup, Hope headed back to her cabin to pull together some last minute items that she wanted to put in her saddlebag, like a toothbrush and toothpaste. The day had turned in to a beauty. The green hills and distant mountains met bright blue skies with only a wisp of a cloud passing by every now and then. And the temperature was in the seventies—perfect weather for riding. A long ride was just what she needed to get her mind off of last night—off both the attack and the fact that she had made love to Calder. For someone who had sworn off cops, she wasn't doing too good.

She stepped inside the cabin and froze. It was a mess—her clothes were scattered all about the cabin. She had to shake her head and think back—but no, it wasn't this way when she left. Someone had been in here going through her things. She was shocked and horrified, and felt as though she had been violated. Again.

What the heck was going on here? Who was trying to make her life miserable? Was it Angela? She had threatened her this morning, but would she be foolish enough to act on that threat?

Hope slowly crossed the room and began to collect her clothing, only to find that several items had been torn up. Or slashed by a knife.

Her pulse quickened as she moved about the small cabin, searching to see if anything was missing and assessing the damage. The gauze blouse she had worn last night had gaping holes in it, along with several other shirts and sweaters she had brought with her. Her makeup and personal items that were on her dresser were strewn across the floor in the bedroom, as though someone had taken their hand across the top of the dresser making a clean sweep, sending everything tumbling to the floor.

How could this be happening? Why was this happening? She was positive she had locked the door when she left this morning. And no one else had a key, except the office and Calder. But it couldn't be Calder—he had left early this morning with Sam and Justin. But he did have the only other key. And last night, he was by her side right after she had gotten hit. How could he have been so close and not seen anyone—unless he . . . No. That was insane. Why would he want to harm her? It didn't make sense. None of it made sense. Overwhelmed with fear and question, she collapsed on the sofa in tears.

Now what should she do—should she pack her things and leave before anything worse happens, or go ahead with her plans for the overnight ride? She had to find out who was doing this to her. She had to know if it was Calder. Wiping the tears from her face, she picked up her belongings and stuffed them in a drawer. She would go on the ride and not tell anyone what happened. It would be her secret—hers and the person who had done this. And she was determined to find out who it was.

Hope met up with Susan at the corral, already brushing down her horse and getting ready to saddle up.

"I'm glad to see you decided to come along. Is John going in to the rodeo?" Hope asked.

"No. He decided to wait until tomorrow night and take me with him. Tonight he's just going to take it easy. He's planning on joining a group drumming up a poker game for tonight. I just asked him not to bet our house!" Susan laughed as she continued, "you know, he doesn't exactly have a poker face!"

Hope led Roman out of the corral, tied him loosely to the rail, and walked over to the tack room porch for a brush and hoof pick. She hesitated at the door, the vision of last night flashing in her mind. She had to shake this feeling of fear that was tightening its grip on her.

"Hope! Heads up!" Susan called to her friend, and motioned in the direction of the barns and creek.

Looking up she saw what Susan was talking about. Walking down from the Saloon was Angela, and she was heading in their direction.

Brushing Roman with deep long strokes, Hope kept her eye on the figure moving toward them. "Do you think she's coming on the overnight?" she asked, looking under Roman's head.

"God I hope not. I was looking forward to this. But if Roger and Joe went, you can bet she's not far behind." Susan smirked.

"I feel sorry for her Susan, I really do. She is just really hung up on someone who seems to care less. I blame Roger for part of this too—he doesn't seem to take the action necessary to end it. Fatal attraction or not." Hope was more concerned with the effect this was having on little Joe. "If it's as bad as he says why has he waited so long to take out a restraining order?"

"You may have something there." Susan grunted as she lifted the heavy saddle on to Flying Spot's back. He danced to the side before settling down, allowing Susan to tighten the girth.

Angela walked by them without saying a word. She headed straight to the tack room and returned with a wrangler, following close behind, holding her tack.

Susan and Hope exchanged a glance and rolled their eyes. Such a prima donna!

"You girls getting saddled up for the afternoon trek to the overnight?" the wrangler asked as he entered the corral for Angela's horse.

"Yes sir," Hope replied, keeping one eye on Angela and the other on the wrangler. It seemed as though the wrangler couldn't keep his eyes off Angela, and was going out of his way to do everything for her. Angela stood back and applied lipstick while her horse was being groomed and saddled.

"Do you all know each other?" the wrangler asked?

"Sure do." answered Angela. "But it's OK if we don't socialize isn't it? I'd much rather spend my time talking to you," she added coyly. The young wrangler beamed with the attention she was giving him. Susan and Hope once again exchanged a look of disbelief.

"What's your name?" Hope asked the wrangler.

"Paul. Paul Hoge, ma'am. I'll be escorting you ladies to the overnight campsite. You're saddle bags are already loaded with water and snacks for the ride. So as soon as everyone is ready to head out, we'll be on our way."

They headed east, back through the ranch road, past the cabins, and into open fields. Angela rode behind Paul, Susan and Hope followed. The horses galloped across the field, and then picked their way along a narrow trail carved through the high grasses. Before entering into the wooded hill country, Paul pulled up to make a check of his riders.

"Everyone OK? Any girths need to be tightened, now's the time to do it." He barked orders to the group as his horse danced in circles. "Are you OK miss Angela?"

"Oh yes. I'm fine. You don't have to stop on my account. I'm an accomplished rider." Angela said, her speech dripping in affected southern accent. She was really playing up to the young wrangler.

Hope tied the leather straps of her hat under her chin and let it fall to her back. Riding in the shelter of towering pines, she no longer needed protection from the sun. And she loved the feel of the wind blowing through her hair. The ride was helping; it was getting her mind off the vision of her ransacked cabin.

The group wound their way along an old trail—stepping lightly through rocky areas littered with fallen timber. It was much cooler in the forest. The trail climbed steadily, forcing the riders to lean forward in the saddle to help their horses navigate the steep slope. The top of the slope opened onto a mesa—a mesa that seemed to go on forever, making a seamless transition to bright blue sky and grand vistas. They pulled up their horses and stopped to enjoy the view. A grove of low growing trees offered shade and a hitching post for the horses.

"You want to make certain to anchor your horse to something, cause you sure don't want him to run off and leave you this far from the ranch. It's a long walk," Paul joked as the girls dismounted and tied their horses to low hanging limbs.

Hope stretched and shook out her legs. They had been riding for about two hours and it was time for a break. Untying the rawhide laces, she reached into her saddlebag to see what had been packed. Energy bars, trail mix, beef jerky and bottled water were on the menu. Hope chose the trail mix and a bottle of water. She walked out into the mesa, soaking up the sun and breathing in the energy of her surroundings. Susan joined her friend.

Angela watched them with intense interest.

"It's pretty amazing up here isn't it?" asked Susan. They stood side by side taking in the beauty. "So far so good with Miss Angela. I wonder if she is so bold with every guy?"

"I'm sure it's her way of practicing her techniques. Look at them," Hope said, glancing in their direction. "Poor Paul—he's young enough to think she's really interested. Just wait until they get to campsite and Angela zooms in on Roger."

"Bye. Bye. Paul," said Susan, shaking her head.

"OK ladies. Let's mount up and get riding. We've got some ground to cover," Paul shouted across the mesa. As they walked back to their horses, Hope watched Angela and wondered if she could be her assailant, but dismissed it because of her size. She was shorter than Hope, and for some reason, Hope just felt sorry for her. All of the talk of Angela possibly being involved with Judy's wreck had disturbed Hope. She was too obsessed with Roger to have had anything to do with a hit and run. They had to be mistaken.

The brief break did wonders for the group. They loped across the open mesa, meeting up with herds of cattle along the way. Paul directed them down away from the mesa, back into wooded trails, heading north, and then pulled up short at a double ditch ahead of them.

"Be careful here. Your horse may want to jump the ditch, but the safest way to cross is to guide you horse down into the ditches at an angle and back up. We'll do it one at a time."

"Looks more like a double canyon than ditch," Susan exclaimed, looking down into a ten to fifteen foot ravine.

"The storms have really done some rearranging of mother nature up here." Paul said, guiding his horse sideways down into the ditch, then stepping onto the other side. His horse leaped up onto the ledge separating the two ditches. "Let me cross this, and then you follow, one by one. Hang on to your horses mane and lean into him as he comes up the ditch," Paul was rightfully concerned for his charges. The terrain in front of them was treacherous.

Angela went next. Her horse balked at going down into the ravine, but finally moved ahead. As her horse lurched up the other side, Angela lost her stirrup and almost fell. She regained her balance on the ridge, then executed the next ridge with ease.

Then it was Hope's turn. Roman stepped cautiously down into the muddy ravine. With each step, the big horse sank into the mud and slid, making the next step even more dangerous. Leaping to the other side to begin the steep incline, Roman stumbled and fell to his knees. Hope's heart was in her throat as she grabbed Roman's mane, leaned forward, and gave him his head. He was off his knees and lunging up the incline within seconds. At the second ditch, he balked. Hope could tell that he wanted to jump the ditch and positioned the big horse to get the best footing. She leaned into him and again gave him his head. He was in the air and cleared the ditch with room to spare.

"Don't follow me," Hope called out to Susan. "Go down a few yards before you try to cross. But be careful, it's real muddy."

Before Susan could redirect Flying Spot to a less traveled area, they were on their way down the ravine. His hooves sank deep into the mire, making each step difficult. Susan held on to his mane and saddle horn as the paint considered the transition to the incline and appeared triumphantly on the ledge between the ravines. But stepping down into the second ravine he lost his footing and stumbled. He was down on his knees, stuck in the mud.

"Give him his head," Paul shouted to Susan, the look of fear on her face.

"He's stuck, I don't think he can move," Susan hollered back.

"He can move, he's just trying to figure out how."

With that, the horse lunged forward and out of the mud. As he emerged out of the ravine Susan was hanging sideways in the saddle, and with his last push up and over the ridge, Susan fell to the ground, and hollered out in pain. It was her wrist—she had braced herself in the fall and had twisted it. Hope quickly dismounted and tied Roman to a nearby tree. She was at Susan's side the same time as Paul.

"Oh my God, Hope. I think I broke something." Susan cried. She was trying to sit up and with every move she cried out in pain. "Oh geez, it's my wrist, I can't move it. I think I broke it!" Susan writhed in pain, tears streamed down her face. "Oh Hope, I can't believe I did this. Poor Flying Spot—is he OK?"

"Your horse is fine Susan, he made it out fine and is patiently waiting for you to climb back on, but I don't think you're ready for that. Now hold still while I look at your hand." Once again Hope was calling on her nursing skills. With gentle caution, she poked and prodded amid gasps of pain from her friend.

"You look like you know what you're doing," Susan said, gritting her teeth to keep from crying out in pain.

"I'm a registered nurse, just not practicing," Hope stated.

"Thank God for that!" replied Susan.

Paul gathered sticks that could be used as a makeshift splint and pulled a long sleeve t-shirt out of his saddlebag, he also retrieved a bottle of water for Susan.

"Always prepared," he said, beaming, as he waved the shirt and water in the air. Angela stood off to the side, annoyed with the delay and the fact that she was no longer the center of his attention.

Susan grit her teeth as Paul and Hope secured her wrist using the sticks and t-shirt to make a splint and sling.

"We'll have to head back to the ranch right away. It will be slow going, but we should be there before nightfall," Paul said to the group as Susan rested against a tree.

"I can't go back to the ranch," Hope said, suddenly realizing spending the night alone in her cabin while most of the guests were on the overnight was not where she wanted to be. And anyway, she had to talk to Calder, she had to find out if he had any knowledge of what happened in her cabin—and she forgot the most important thing—she had to tell him about Jane Doe. "I've got a message I have to deliver to Calder, it's an emergency," she said, standing up, starting to pace. She rubbed her arms, feeling a sudden chill after the excitement of Susan's injury.

"And Roger is expecting me. If I don't show up he'll come looking for me. I know it. He gets crazy when I'm not around." Angela was becoming agitated with the thought of having to go back to the ranch.

"Whoa, wait a minute ladies. I'm the wrangler here, and I'm responsible for *all* of you," Paul stated, as though his sense of responsibility also meant that his word was final.

"You are responsible for us as long as we put ourselves in your care. However, we are adults, and can do as we choose." Hope spoke with authority, hoping that Paul would give in.

"I can't go in two directions at once, and that lady, she needs some medical attention, quick."

"We know Paul. So why don't you ride back to the ranch with Susan, and give Angela and I directions to the campsite. I'm sure you can give good directions to the camp site, can't you?" she asked, trying to chide him into going along with her idea.

"Of course I can. It's almost a straight shot from here. At least, it's not that hard to find." He took off his hat and scratched his head. He was obviously concerned about what to do.

"I need to get to the campsite Paul. And if you can't take me there and be with me, at least you can tell me how to get there. If you do, I promise to give you a hug tomorrow when we get back!" Angela said in her most affected southern accent.

It almost made Hope sick. It was bad enough leaving her friend with a broken wrist to ride back to the ranch alone with Paul. But Susan understood, and thank goodness John would be there to take her to the hospital. Hope had to talk to Calder. She had to tell him about Jane Doe.

After kicking the dirt with his boots for a short time, and him-hawing around, Paul finally agreed to give Hope and Angela directions to ride to the campsite.

Hope held on to Flying Spot while Susan stepped up on Paul's back, and carefully mounted her horse. She gathered the reins in her left hand, while the makeshift t-shirt sling held her right arm close to her chest. Yes, it would be a slow ride back. They had to go about a mile out of their way just to get around the ditches, but there was no way Susan was going to attempt to go back over them.

The sun was high in the sky when the group split. Hope and Angela headed north through the woods. They followed the trail, Hope leading the way. Actually, it was more like Roman was leading the way. He had traveled these trails for years, and by giving him his head, they trotted through the trees without concern.

The forest opened into a field, black and white cattle scattered about, grazing contentedly, pausing occasionally to watch the riders pass through. The riders crossed the field toward a shed that Paul had told them about. The trail continued on behind it. As they re-entered the forest, they pulled up their horses. They heard voices in the distance.

"Where are they coming from?" Hope turned her question to Angela?

"I don't know. I can't even tell what they're saying. Let's just keep going, there not looking for us," Angela said, intent on getting to the campsite and Roger.

"They might need help. We need to signal back to them," Hope replied, keeping Roman in check. "OVER HERE," she shouted. "OVER HERE."

The woods became suddenly silent, and the events of the past two days had Hope on edge. Was someone following her?

Angela began slowly walking her horse down the trail. "I tell you we need to keep going. We're never going to get there if you stop to talk with everyone along the way. They're probably just out riding like we're supposed to be doing," Angela replied in a huff, then kicked her horse and disappeared around a twist in the trail.

"OK. I guess they don't want company. According to Paul we need to follow this trail through the woods for about another hour, then it should bring us to a clearing and another out building." Hope said to herself, reining Roman around and into a fast trot to catch up with Angela.

The fresh scent of pine and dampness of the woods after heavy rains combined into a heady musky scent. The horses carefully picked their way through stone and bog. It was an eerie beauty, the forest heavy with moisture, blanketed with pine and limbs giving shelter to squirrels, raccoon, and other small creatures that made their home there.

The canopy of trees became less dense, and the sunlight streamed onto the trail. The late afternoon sun was strong; Hope wiped her brow and straightened her cowboy hat. She wanted to talk to Angela about their encounter at breakfast, and her insinuation that she was interested in Roger. If she only knew that was the farthest thing from her mind. If anything, she felt sorry for the whole lot of them, Roger, Angela, Roger's wife, but most of all little Joe. For a child to be mixed up in affairs and torn between parents had to be torture for such a young guy. It's hard enough to make sense of that when you're grown, much less a child.

Her thoughts drifted back to their trip to the ice cream parlor. Joe's freckles seemed to come alive with happiness as he and Calder shared stories and ice cream. He gobbled up the attention Calder gave him like he did his ice cream, attention not given in a doting way, but as one guy to another—like a big brother. Calder was good with kids—it didn't take her long to figure that out. Heck, he was good with just about everyone. Bottom line, he knew who he was, he was comfortable in his own skin, and because of that, he was easy to connect with.

She didn't believe that he was responsible for the shovel incident or ransacking her cabin—but he is the only one she can connect to both events. And come to think of it—if he had headed up the mountain to his cabin after leaving the airport the night of the accident, he would have encountered the accident before she and Justin came on it. Maybe he was protecting his sister—and trying to cast the guilt on someone else in the area, like Angela. Maybe his sister was responsible for the hit and run and he was trying to cover it up.

Her sense of solving problems told her not to overlook a potential suspect just because of . . . Because of what? Because she liked him? Was she falling for him? Or was it because he was the Chief of Police? Just because he was supposed to be one of the good guys didn't mean he was. She had been exposed to enough cops in her lifetime to know that not all were in it for the right reasons. It did make a good cover and cast doubt on others. At this point, she wasn't sure what to believe.

Interesting enough, among all this mystery and confusion, this past week had allowed Hope the opportunity to once again be comfortable with herself. No airs, no pretenses; what you see is what you get. She liked that feeling. She had forgotten how right it felt to be at home in her own skin. Was it the vacation, the mountains, the case, or just that time in her life, a transition point? Heck, she was thirty-one years old, and it was time she found out who she was and what she wanted to do with her life.

Prior to coming to Wyoming, she lacked direction and responsibility. Her only responsibility in Charlotte was to get up and go to work in the morning and pay rent, and lately she had been having problems doing that. And as far as emotional responsibilities, she had made a point not to have them. Heck, she didn't even own a gold fish—and had managed to kill just about every plant in her apartment.

But emotional responsibilities were all around her here. Everywhere she turned, the people that were affecting her the most were those with responsibility they took pride in fulfilling. Nursing had once provided her that outlet, she knew she made a difference in other's lives, and looked forward to fulfilling that responsibility every day. It had been her drug of choice; it was the high that kept her coming back for more. She hadn't realized how much she missed that feeling until now, in Wyoming. The mountains had some how helped her peel back layers of life to find out who she really was.

But what about Calder, what role did he play in this? She was certainly attracted to him, last night was proof positive of that. She smiled to herself at the thought of him, his presence was a comfort to her mind, her body—all her senses. Just being near him had seemed right, but then again, she hadn't been too lucky with her choice in men in the past. Why should now be any different. Was last night real, or just part of his plan to get her to trust him, so he could blow smoke on the real person responsible for the hit and run—his sister?

Over an hour passed before the trail opened up on to a meadow spattered with wildflowers. The shed offered some much needed shade and a water trough for the horses. Hope slid off the big roan horse and led him over to the trough. He sucked in the water like a camel, one very long gulp that seemed to last for several minutes.

"I think I need some water too," Hope said, trying to strike up conversation with Angela. She opened her saddlebag and removed a power bar and bottle of water. It felt good to get out of the saddle, but even better to get something to drink. She led Roman away from the shed to the grassy area; Angela watched her every move.

The varying beauty of the meadows amazed Hope—each vista ever changing, always breathtaking, yet never predictable. Snowcapped mountains seemed almost touchable now, and even though the sun was still high in the sky, she could feel the thinness of the air. A hawk soared overhead, catching downdrafts, effortlessly negotiating the wind patterns of the mountains. Hope watched him maneuver through his environment, wishing she knew her strengths as well as the hawk knew his.

"Well no time like to present to clear the air," Hope told herself, taking a long drink from her water bottle.

Angela looked away as soon as Hope made eye contact.

"Angela," Hope said, "about this morning. I'm not sure what that was all about." Suddenly her legs felt like they were going to buckle under her.

"No? Well let me make it a bit clearer." Angela jerked her horse's head up away from his snack and stepped closer to Hope. Her eyes narrowed with anger. "I don't take lightly to women falling all over Roger. He's mine and I plan on keeping it that way. So stay away from him and his son or you'll regret it." She snapped.

Hope shook her head trying to clear her vision. A bead of sweat broke out on her forehead. "But you've got it all wrong. I'm not interested in Roger. What ever gave you that idea?" she asked, the contorted look on Angela's face was starting to concern Hope, or was it her eyes. She suddenly felt faint and weak. The water bottle fell out of her hand.

"You're all alike," she hissed. "Blondes! You think that you can get away with anything by playing the dumb blonde. Men might fall for that trick, but I sure don't. I can see through you. You want to ruin everything! Well, you can't. I worked hard to get Roger, and I'm not giving him up to you, Judy, or anyone!"

Angela was on top of her before she realized what was happening. Hope felt the force of Angela's body crash into her, knocking her off balance and to the ground. Her head was spinning and her vision blurred. Her attempt to get back on her feet was thwarted by dizziness. Had she hit her head on something?

"Judy?" Hope whispered, trying to speak, trying to make sense of what Angela had said before her world began spinning and drifting away. Where was she? Why was she so tired?

"Stupid bitch. I'm not Judy. Judy's lying in a hospital in a coma. Perhaps you won't be so lucky." Angela stood over Hope's limp body. "Come on honey. Don't give up on me yet. Let's get you back on your horse." Angela said, pulling Hope by one arm, dragging her over to the shed. Hope's mind was telling her to stand up, and her legs were trying, but she couldn't. She couldn't move, she couldn't see, she couldn't make sense of what was happening to her.

"Judy?" she asked again. This time her question was answered with a kick to the ribs.

"There, if you won't fall off your horse I'll make it look like you did," she said, kicking her again.

Hope lay curled up in the dirt, clutching and protecting her already broken ribs. It was difficult to breath. Why couldn't she breathe? It had to be her ribs. God it hurt so bad to breathe.

"Help me. Please. Help . . ." her voice trailed off into a whisper. Her head fell to the side and her eyes rolled back in her head.

Angela watched her for a few moments knowing she should be dead in a little while. Hope's body lay there, motionless. Angela picked up her foot and kicked her one more time for good measure. "That's for my mother," she said, and turned away from Hope. She got back up on her horse and headed for the campsite, never once looking back.

CHAPTER 16

CALDER LEANED INTO the stream, cupped his hands, and splashed water over his face for the third time that afternoon. The campsite was set and the morning riders had arrived and settled in. He was waiting for the afternoon riders—one in particular.

Hope had occupied Calder's mind all morning. The slow motion of the packhorses reminded him of the slow burn that had been building in him since boarding that plane in Salt Lake City. Persistent. As were his thoughts. The sight of Hope with morning light streaming in casting hints of gold and wheat on her hair, the softness of her face, and the truth in her spirit. He had fallen for the city slicker and knew he was in trouble. She would be going back to North Carolina soon, and North Carolina and Wyoming were worlds apart. Beyond the miles, beyond the cultural differences—it was like a never-ending ocean when he thought of how far she would be from him. He couldn't attempt to cross it; he knew he'd drown. He'd tried once before. It was like a spell had been cast on him as a child—dare he venture from the Elliott kingdom he would wither away and die. He wondered if the same applied to Hope. But she was light and life in Wyoming; he couldn't imagine her being any brighter, or any more charming in Charlotte. He wanted to be with her—not only in the biblical sense, but just with her. Being close to her energized him and brought him comfort. Being with her just seemed right.

His mother used to always tell him that he'd know it when he met the right girl. He thought he knew it when he met Kelly, but this was nothing compared to what he felt then. This scared him. He knew it—but . . . He couldn't think beyond next week, beyond the end of her vacation. She was on loan to him—a gift from the Gods. Maybe the spell that had been cast on him was an evil spell—he would find his goddess but not be able to be with her. He would know heaven on earth but only for a brief time. Life really was cruel.

The clip-clop sound of a horse trotting up brought him back to the moment. But it was only one horse. He turned in the direction of the incoming rider, wondering who had stumbled upon their campsite. Outside riders often happened upon the group—and they would invite them in to rest for a while. Friends, acquaintances—most of the folks packing through the Big Horn Mountains were known to Calder and Sam. Either they were neighbors, or return tourists. It was hard to experience the Big Horns and turn your back on them forever. Return visitors made up half the tourists, and at least a quarter of the local population during the spring and summer months. Calder shaded his eyes with his hand, squinting into the afternoon sun. One rider. A woman.

The stream was a distance from the campsite, and as Calder walked toward the tents, he caught a glimpse of red hair. "Angela," he said under his breath. "How did she find her way out here by herself?" He walked up to her as she was talking to Sam.

"Roger and Joe are out fishing," Sam said to the redhead.

"What do you mean they're out fishing?" Her tone of voice was less than pleasant. She appeared to be agitated. Sam looked up at Calder approaching them and called out, "Can you show Ms. Angela the direction of the watering hole where Roger and Joe are catching dinner?" Sam asked, in his friendly easy-going tone.

"Sure." Calder said, reaching out for the reins to Angela's horse. "Here, let me take your horse over to the corral first. Then I'll show you where they are." Calder knew his priorities, and the horse ranked much higher than Angela.

He took his time unsaddling the gelding and brushing him down. After turning him into the corral, he turned his attention to Angela. She leaned against the chuck wagon, not speaking to other guests or socializing in any way. Strange lady.

"Come on. They're down here." Calder motioned to her and headed down a wooded trail.

"How far is it?"

"About a mile."

She stopped in the middle of the trail and put her hands on her hips. "You've got to be kidding me. A mile? Why don't you run on down there and tell him I'm here, OK?" Angela said, flipping her hair in obvious disdain over walking a mile.

"No ma'am. If you want to see Roger, you can follow me and I'll show you where he's fishing. If you don't, then I'm not going to waste my time walking down there. He'll be back before dark." Calder glared; she was the most belligerent, selfish woman he had ever met. There was nothing attractive about her, at least to him. She wore way too much makeup to be out in the middle of the Big Horn Mountains on an overnight ride. Her jeans were way too tight; they must have been real uncomfortable. Maybe that's why she was so unpleasant. He waited for her to reply. Hearing none, he turned and started walking back to the campsite.

"OK. You win," she said, her attitude spilled out ahead of her words. "Lead on."

The trail wound through the woods, and the campsite seemed miles away. Calder stopped to wait for Angela to catch up to him, wondering how she had found them.

"How'd you get up here all by yourself? Lucky guess?" Calder asked, wondering about Hope.

"No. Paul Hoge, he's one of the wranglers, he directed us out here." She replied, still walking toward the spot where Calder leaned against a pine.

"Us?" he asked, his interest piqued.

"Yes, me, Hope, and somebody named Susan. We all left the ranch together."

"So where are they?" Calder asked, pushing himself away from the pine, ready to pounce and concerned with Hope's safety.

"Well we got off track and ended up having to cross some treacherous ravines. You know, that wrangler could have killed me. The ranch should give me something for the trouble he put me through." Angela said, rubbing her hands on her tight jeans.

"That didn't answer my question Angela. Where are they?" He said, raising his voice. "*Where's Hope?*"

"Susan had an accident crossing the ravine, and hurt her wrist. Probably broke it," she said calmly. Calder relaxed for a moment. Hope must have gone back to the ranch with Susan.

"Paul took her back to the ranch, and gave Hope and I directions here. We started off together, but Hope kept riding faster than I could go, and we got separated. She should already be here, she was ahead of me." Angela said nonchalantly, and walked by Calder, and on down the path.

Calder didn't believe a word she said, but let her walk away. She obviously didn't care what happened to Hope—giving him even more reason to believe that Angela was the person he had followed that night. Angela was the one behind the shovel. But he didn't have any proof yet and no need to waste valuable time trying to get the truth out of her.

He raced back to the campsite in search of his horse and Sam. He found both at the corral and filled Sam in on the particulars as he saddled up. In a matter of minutes, Calder was back on the trail in the direction Angela had ridden in from. Jake emerged from the woods and barked with enthusiasm. Calder rode hard out of the camp, quickly putting distance between him and the campsite.

They covered several miles before Calder slowed his horse, and Jake caught up to him. Riding hard was not going to help him find Hope. Did she lose her way? That was hard to imagine since Angela had found the campsite. Maybe her horse got spooked and she was thrown, or fell. Anything could happen out here, and it wasn't safe for her to be out here alone. He tried to recall what Angela had said, and it didn't make sense to him. Last night when they were talking about the case, Hope had mentioned wanting to talk to Angela, feeling sorry for her. Why would she have ridden off alone?

Calder decided to dismount, walk slow, and scan the area for signs. He looked all around the forest for anything that looked out of place. And he listened. He listened to the sounds of squirrels, birds, and other animals that lived in the area. Their sounds were ingrained in his psyche, like the hum of a refrigerator at home. He tried to isolate them and block them out, but heard nothing unique.

Jake followed close behind, stopping when Calder stopped, soon picking up the fact that Calder was hunting. Jake began to inspect the area with his nose as Calder watched the big black dog work. Realizing Jake wanted to join the hunt, he pulled Hope's flannel shirt from his saddlebag. It had fallen to the floor with his the night before, and when he reached for his shirt that morning in the dark, he had picked up hers too, and rolled it up into his saddlebag. He knew she would probably need it come nightfall—which wasn't far off.

Before offering it to Jake to get her scent, he gathered it to his face and breathed in the memory of her. The smell of lavender was still there. Good thing he remembered it. If it remained rolled up in there with the other items, it would soon smell more like beef jerky than lavender, and that wouldn't help. He took in her scent once more before holding it down for the big black dog.

"Jake. Find Hope," he commanded.

Jake barked and danced around. He sniffed at the shirt again and barked louder—staring at Calder as though he was speaking to him. In a way he was. They started back down the trail. Jake cutting in and out of trees, his nose to the ground. For a retriever it seemed odd that he loved to hunt with his nose to the ground. Retrievers are visual dogs. But Jake loved any kind of hunting; it was the game of finding things that he enjoyed most, and Calder loved the look of surprise on Jake's face when he found the origin of the scent.

Calder remounted his horse and walked him slowly through the thick woods. His eyes searched left and right, trying to discern anything out of the ordinary. He wished he knew what she had worn. Did she have on her vest, or was she wearing one of her long sleeved t-shirts that he loved to see her in, that accented all the right curves.

"Find Hope," he commanded again, reminding Jake of his mission. The pair scoured the area. It was possible that Hope had arrived at the campsite while Calder was out searching for her. He prayed that was the case, but would not quit looking until nightfall made it impossible to see.

The sun was starting to set and the temperature quickly dropped. So far, Calder and Jake had been unlucky in their search. It was as though Jake hadn't been able to pick up any trace of her—like she hadn't been there at all. Was that possible? But according to Angela Hope had gone ahead of her. How far ahead before she got off the trail? Again, why would she venture off the trail? The questions flooded his analytical mind. But there were no answers.

He decided to continue on until they reached the meadow area. Maybe there he could get a better fix on where they got separated. That is, if he arrived before dark.

Jake began making a wider sweep in his search for the scent on the shirt. He trotted along, nose to the ground, tail straight back, crossing fallen limbs and rock formations, diligent in his mission.

The lighting in the woods changed, and in the twilight he thought he saw a clearing ahead.

It was then that Jake started barking. Frantically.

Calder slid off his horse and followed the sounds of the bark. Was it Hope? Had Jake found Hope?

The dog was barking at a bush behind an old shed. Calder's disappointment at the thought of Jake treeing a coon was soon exchanged for a shot of adrenaline when he spotted a boot in the bushes.

"Hope. Is that you?" he said as he ran toward the spot. Jake was dancing now, happy and excited for doing his job.

"Good boy. Good Boy!" Calder said emphatically, praising his friend for finding her.

It was Hope, but she wasn't moving. She was unconscious and appeared dirty and disheveled. She looked as though she had been in a fight. Her face was covered with dust, dirt marks on her shirt. He checked her pulse—very weak; but she was still breathing.

He was afraid to move her. Did she have a head or neck injury? It didn't appear so—but dare he chance it?

"Hope! Hope! Can you hear me?" he spoke in a loud voice, trying to get some sort of response. Nothing. He ripped at the bushes, trying to clear the area so he could get next to her to see if anything was broken. Jake stood watching, waiting for his find to wake up and pat him. He had a long wait.

Calder ran back to his horse and pulled a flashlight and some water from his saddlebag. He used the flannel shirt with Hope's scent to gently wipe the dirt from her face. After checking the back of her head for lumps or cuts, he gently rolled her on her back. Her arm fell to the ground, lifeless. He tucked the flannel shirt under her chin, and added his jacket as a half blanket, trying to keep her warm.

If she had fallen and had a concussion, he should be able to get some response from her, a moan or something. But there was none, and with the flashlight it didn't appear as though she had any contusions from falling, other than a few scratches on her face and neck from the bushes. It was like she was drugged.

Calder stood up and flashed his light around the area. Odd, there didn't appear to be any prints other than his own in the area. If she had been thrown from her horse, there should have been hoof marks. The ground was wet enough from all the rain that imprints should still be visible, but it appeared as though the covering of pine needles had not been touched. And this seemed an odd area for her to be, unless she had ridden back behind the shed to find some privacy. Girls were funny about relieving themselves in the middle of the woods—the animals didn't mind but they always had to get behind a bush or a tree. Funny.

Jake took hesitant steps toward Hope, sniffed, and then licked her face as if he knew something was wrong. Soulful brown eyes turned to Calder and then back to Hope before stretching out next to her, his square head resting on her arm, offering protection.

"Good boy. You stay there and guard Hope. I'm going to see if I can find her horse, and then figure out how I'm going to get her back to camp," Calder said, knowing the most dangerous thing he could do was move her, but he had to. They were out in the wilderness—no way an ambulance could get back here. A helicopter maybe—but then he'd have to ride all night to get help, and he wasn't going to leave her. No. He had to take her to the camp; at least there he had lanterns and blankets. He could keep her warm and safe until first light—then begin the trek back to the ranch and a doctor. But maybe, with some luck and a prayer, she would regain consciousness. Damn, he wished he knew what happened, maybe then he could figure out how to help her.

The meadow grass was already becoming damp from the night, and glistened like silver as the flashlight swept across it in search of Roman. He knew the big roan wouldn't be far off; the grass in this meadow was lush and high—enough to hold any horse's attention for several hours. He spotted him in the distance and turned off the light so not to frighten him.

"Roman! Here boy," he called out, more to get his attention and let him know he was coming toward him than expecting the horse to walk up to him. A whinny in the distance let Calder know he had heard him. Calder's own horse, tied by the shed, answered back, and Roman started walking in Calder's direction.

After securing Roman by the shed, he went back to check on Hope. Jake was still in the same position, which told Calder there was no change in her condition. He knelt down by her side.

"Hang in there, Hope. I don't know how this happened, but I'm here now and everything's going to be alright." He stoked her face and hair praying that somehow she knew he was there, that he'd take care of her. Nothing would ever harm her again. He kissed her hand.

Once again he commanded Jake to be on guard, but that wasn't necessary—Jake wasn't moving.

A search of the area turned up two strong saplings to serve as a makeshift litter. He used the rope from his saddle to weave a hammock between the two saplings, and attached it to the back of Roman's saddle. He would have preferred carrying her right behind his own horse, but by tying the litter to Roman and leading him, he could bring both horse and rider back to camp.

After getting the horses and litter arranged, he went back to get Hope. Jake watched as Calder carefully scooped her up in his arms and carried her to the litter.

"You'll be alright Hope. Everything is going to be alright." He whispered repeatedly as he carefully knelt down next to the litter and placed her in it.

Using long sleeved t-shirts he found in her saddlebag, he tied them under her arms and over her chest to secure her in the litter, and used his belt around her legs to provide additional security. He mounted his horse and ever so slowly the procession began moving into the forest, heading for the campsite. The soft padding of horses' hooves against the damp forest floor was methodical and soothing to Calder. It had a way of bringing him back to the moment, keeping him focused on the trail and their slow but constant progress. He knew it would be like this tomorrow and wasn't sure if the wagon would be any safer or quicker in taking Hope back to the ranch. Either way—they would have to take the old logging road. The trails through the forest were rocky and laden with fallen limbs—no path for a litter. He stopped every so often, shining his flashlight on Hope, making certain his most precious package was still in tact.

Halfway back to the camp Calder heard someone in the forest. He pulled up and hollered, "Who goes there?"

"It's me, Sam, and Justin," the reply was distant but welcomed.

Sam and Justin pulled their horses to a stop and watched in the moonlight as the procession wound through the forest toward them.

"What happened?" asked Sam, dismounting and tying his horse to a tree. In three strides he was by Calder and surveying the situation.

Calder dismounted and began talking as soon as his feet touched the ground. Sam knew him well enough to know he was upset—the only time Calder talked fast was when he was nervous, or extremely upset, neither of which happened very often. For as long as Sam had known Calder, his methodical mind almost always led his emotions. The last time Sam heard him talk this fast was when his mother was taken by ambulance to the hospital, right before she died.

"I've got to get her to a safe, warm place. I'm sure she'll come around . . . not a mark on her. She was covered in dirt." He rambled on while rechecking the security of Hope's litter. "I can't figure out what happened Sam. The area seemed too clean, like someone had covered it up. I couldn't find a print anywhere. Not animal or human. I checked all around. But it was dark already, and hard to see. I'll have to go back in daylight and look again. Maybe on the way out in the morning."

"Nice looking litter," Sam said, trying to get a word in edgewise and get Calder's mind back on the task of taking Hope to safety. "Don't think any one else could have done any better. Why don't I lead the way and let Justin follow from behind." Sam half-asked, half-told Calder his plan.

The men got back on their horses and fell in line. They rode single file—Sam, Calder, Hope's horse and her litter, Jake remaining right behind Hope, and then Justin. Silence fell on the group as once again the slow methodical sound of horses' hooves padding against the damp forest floor calmed Calder's worried mind and heart.

CHAPTER 17

CAMPFIRE SONGS RESONATED through the night, reminding Calder they were fast approaching the campsite. The singing ceased when the procession arrived. Wranglers and guests joined in to help unsaddle horses, find blankets, and do anything they could to help Calder get Hope situated in his tent. Blankets were carefully folded together for padding under the sleeping bag to soften her bed, while the softest blanket was used as a pillow. His strong arms trembled as he knelt to the floor and placed Hope on the bed, gently moving strands of hair from her face. He picked up her hand in both of his and kissed it. Her breathing was less shallow now, that had to be a good sign. And color seemed to be returning to her face. She was still very pale, but not ashen as she appeared in the forest. Maybe it was his flashlight, or just the horror of finding her unconscious and in such a disheveled state. He still couldn't figure out how she got mud all over her face and in her hair. Questions ran rampant through his mind as he zipped the bag up to her waist, and covered the rest of her with the remaining blanket. He wanted her to have some flexibility to move, in case she came around, and not feel as though she was wrapped like a mummy.

"Jake," he called through the open tent door. The dog's big square head poked through the flap that acted as a door. "You stay in here and guard Hope." He held the flap open for Jake to enter the tent. He made his usual three circles and once again laid along side Hope, his head toward the front of the tent.

"She's resting, and her breathing seems to have improved," Calder said to Sam as he emerged from the tent. "I need to have a little talk with Angela—I don't quite buy the story she told me earlier. Something happened out there and I want to know what it was." The muscle in his jaw tightened as he looked around the camp for Angela. Come to think of it, he didn't noticed her as part of the guests and wranglers that came to help when they arrived back at camp. He spoke to Roger and Joe, but he didn't remember seeing Angela amidst the flurry of excitement getting Hope into the tent.

"You know, in all the years we've been having our overnight rides, nothing like this has ever happened. Oh, we've had our fair share of broken bones and minor scrapes from falls, but that's been the extent of it. We try our best to keep the guests safe." Sam said, his concern for Hope showed on his weathered face. "You really care for her don't you?" Sam asked, putting his hand on Calder's shoulder.

"Is it that obvious? If anything happens to her, I don't know . . . it's all my fault. I never should have gotten her involved in the case. She would have ridden with the morning group if it hadn't been for her wanting to go to town to check on Jane Doe." Calder hung his head in shame. He had welcomed her involvement; it had given him an opportunity to spend time with her without looking like a lovesick schoolboy following her around the ranch.

"She's going to be OK Calder. We'll get her into the hospital in the morning and she'll be OK," his friend said, trying to reinsure him. "Now you need to get something to eat and get some rest. You'll be of no use to her if you don't. It's been a long day."

A bark from inside the tent startled the men. Within seconds Calder was inside the tent. Jake watched his patient intently, and reached his huge paw up to touch Hope on the shoulder, the shoulder that had taken the full force of a shovel just the night before.

She moaned.

It was the first sign of life since he found her hours ago.

"Hope. It's me, Calder. Wake up Hope. Wake up."

He reached for the rag soaking in water, wringed it out and pressed it to her lips.

Again, she moaned.

"Is everything OK in there?" Sam shouted through the tent door.

"Yes, we're OK. You go on and eat Sam; I'm going to stay here. I think maybe she's coming to."

Food and questioning Angela would have to wait until morning—the most important thing right now was Hope; he had to be there for her.

*

Her eyelids were so very heavy, and her head was throbbing. She wanted to reach her hand up to rub her temple but it wouldn't move. She didn't have the strength to move it. Her eyes—so heavy, like they were taped shut. Her mind wandered. Was someone there? Brian? Is that you? There was someone in the distance. Oh if only she could open her eyes or speak. It was like she was in a bubble, or encased in a tomb of fog—thick dense fog with figures moving in the distance—heavy, heavy fog. It was pressing in on her, holding her down. Pressing against her eyelids and head. Boom, boom, the sound inside her head reverberated. Why won't it stop? Maybe it's from the fog. Brian is that you? She tried to lift her arm to wave to him, but couldn't. Oh, where did he go?

"Brian?" she mumbled in the faintest of voices.

Calder reached across and gently stroked her head. "What is it Hope?" he whispered to her. He kept stroking her head, her arm, and holding her hand. He needed that connection as much as he hoped it would help her regain consciousness.

"Brian?" she asked again.

This time Calder understood the name, but had no idea who she was asking for. Not since that first day on the mesa when he found her crying and kissed her, had she even hinted that there might be someone in her life. Even then, she didn't say there was another person, she just said she couldn't get involved. Who is Brian? She mentioned a brother, was his name Brian? No. He was guessing now, and knew better than to think she was calling out for her brother.

"Hope, it's me, Calder," he said, squeezing her hand. This time he felt a twinge of response. Maybe it was just a muscle reflex but he felt it. He raised her hand and held it against his cheek, then kissed it. "It's me, Calder," he said again, hoping for another response.

The fog was thick again, and the figure disappeared. She felt something touch her hand, a feather or a butterfly, but butterflies don't fly in the fog. She couldn't see her hand, what was it that felt so soft? Her eyelids were still weighted down, and the heaviness of the fog was too much for her to cope with. Maybe if she rested now and didn't fight it, it would go away. Yes, maybe if she rested she could open her eyes. She was so tired; so very tired.

*

Calder lay on his side next to her, holding on to her hand. Somehow, off and on through the night, he managed to fall asleep. He checked her forehead again for fever; she was still warm. But the rambling speech and occasional moan indicated she was trying to communicate, whether here or in a dream state. She had called out for Brian several times that night, but never once spoke Calder's name. It shouldn't have bothered him, but it did.

He lay by her, dozing off every so often, holding tight to her hand. With every movement, every noise, he woke and checked on her. Checking her forehead for a temperature, calling her name to see if she would respond. And it was late into the night, when the camp was sound asleep, that he told her the story of the snow gods again. But this time she was the trapper, stranded and lost in the night. Calder was the one waiting for her safe return, but only the snow gods could make it happen. The snow gods could make anything happen. And as he retold the story, he prayed to the snow gods, prayed that Hope would return to him. Prayed for her safe recovery, and looking up through the skylight in his tent, he began counting.

"Judy . . . ," a soft voice called in the night.

He had been counting, "twenty, twenty-one, . . ." when he woke to a soft sound. He studied her face again. Had she spoken his name?

"Hope? Wake up Hope," he said. Whispering her name like a prayer; and it was sometime during the night he realized her name was a prayer. Hope. She truly was his hope—his hope for tomorrow and his future. Wherever she went she spread hope—it was in every word she spoke, every action. She had brought hope back into his life. Hope that he could love again, that his heart could once again welcome love. But most of all that his heart would once again give love. That is what he feared most—giving love, sharing love. And it was Hope he wanted to share it with.

"Calder," she whispered. Her speech was raspy and barely audible. But this time, he heard his name. He squeezed her hand and pulled it close to his chest.

"I'm here Hope. I'm here. I'm going to get you out of here, you're going to be OK." He was thrilled that she was talking, but she still had not opened her eyes, and was soon back in a state of deep sleep.

*

The fog remained low and heavy, but not as thick as before. She could command her hand to move, and after a bit, it would move. But it made her so tired. So very, very tired. Every attempt to move through the fog was such an effort, so exhausting. Her muscles ached and they refused to obey. She still could not open her eyes. The fog was like cement, sealing them shut. Maybe she would never see again. If only she could open her eyes, then she would know who was there. But someone was there. It wasn't Brian; he was gone. It was someone else—in the fog. He was strong and real, and was there to clear the fog. She had a blurred image of him—and felt as though she knew him. He had rescued her before, and came back now to save her. But he scared her. She wanted to reach out to him but wasn't sure if he was there to help her, or had brought the fog. She was tired again, and needed more sleep. She'd think about it later. Later.

*

Daybreak couldn't come soon enough. Calder dressed in silence and gathered supplies as the sun began to send shafts of gold and orange through the morning sky. Justin approached Calder at the corral; he had decided to go along if for no other reason than moral support. Steam rose from the horses as they saddled up for the long ride back to the ranch. Calder had opted to use the litter he had made the night before, it would be quicker than using the wagon, and this way, he could ride back to the area where he found her, to look at the site during the day. With the roping checked and reknotted, Calder tied it into position behind Roman. Food and water was stored in their saddlebags. The ride back would be slow.

He carefully tucked blankets around her for warmth as he once again positioned Hope on the litter. He didn't want the morning chill to reverse the progress she had made during the night. She was still unconscious, but had spoken several times throughout the night. The names of Brian and Judy were fresh on his mind—who are they?

Calder and Justin headed out of camp at daybreak with Hope in tow behind. Jake again followed behind, his eyes fixed on Hope and the litter. They made their way through the trail they had brought Hope in on the night before. Calder knew he had to look over the site where he found her before anything or anyone had time to alter it. The group moved slowly through the winding forest trail, and the sun was bright on the meadow as the procession approached and came to a stop. Justin dismounted and tied his horse to a tree, and checked on Hope, making certain she was still secure in the litter.

Calder rode ahead toward the meadow opening, dismounted, and tied his horse away from the shed, not to disturb any tracks other than his own from last night. Each step was deliberate, and before his foot landed he surveyed the area in front of him. It took him some time to cover the area to the bushes behind the shed where he had found Hope. In the morning light, it was easy for him to see that someone had taken a branch and wiped away markings from the ground. He followed the trail of cover-up back toward the meadow, back toward a trail of occasional footsteps mixed with parallel markings that had no break—as though something or someone was being dragged. He bent down and fingered the fresh tracks, then stood and placed his own foot next to the footprint.

"Oh my God," he said out loud. He removed his hat and ran his fingers through black wavy hair. The footprints were that of either a child, woman, or small man. If the drag marks were from Hope, then he doubted the footprints were a child's. That left a woman or small man. And only one person came into his mind. That was a woman with flaming red hair. The one person that said she had last seen Hope in the meadow—riding off ahead of her. That was obviously a lie—but what had happened?

He continued his search of the area, looking for any other clues that might help him pin point the reason. Hoof prints surrounded the area, but as best he could tell there were only two horses that stood nearby. The morning sun bounced off something partially covered in the tall grass, something that beckoned him to examine it closer. It was a water bottle, discarded into the grass. Was it Hope's or had some other rider thrown in there? He picked it up as possible evidence. It was the only thing he could see in the area where Hope originally went down. He continued to survey the area but coming up with nothing, he headed back to his horse.

The sun's glistening rays washed over the meadow grasses, changing the hues and colors. Did he have time to ride back to camp and interview Angela? Should he let her know he suspects she had something to do with Hope's accident? Scenarios played out in his head. His whistle cut through the quiet of the morning. He motioned for Justin to join him in the meadow.

The leather reins fell on the left side of his horse's thick neck turning them west, following the meadow down to the logging road. Hope's safe arrival at the ranch and hospital was his first priority. The ride back to the ranch would give him time to structure his line of questioning for Angela.

*

Once again he was pacing. He didn't know what to do next. His nerves were getting the best of him. He wanted to be with Hope when she regained consciousness, but also had business to take care of. He had to go back to the cabin and search through her belongings to find a number to notify her family. In a way he wanted to wait until the lab reports and x-rays were back and had more information before he called them—to say what? Hope is lying unconscious in a hospital in Wyoming and we have no idea why?

His long strides made short business of pacing the hospital corridor in front of Hope's room. With each pass, he stopped by her door for a quick check. "She is resting well," the doctor said.

Yea, Calder thought to himself—it's the resting that I'm worried about. Why is she unconscious? What happened out there, and was Angela responsible? He had to find out.

A phone at the far end of the hallway beckoned to him.

"Doris? Calder. Listen, something has come up and I'm at the hospital. Yes, I'm OK; there was an accident out at the ranch. So if you need me for anything I'll be here at the hospital off and on throughout the day." Calder spoke at max speed. He barked out a few orders and finally paused long enough for Doris to speak.

"I'm still trying to contact family on your Jane Doe, Judy Longacre."

"What? What did you say?" Calder asked, turning his full attention back to the phone.

"Didn't she tell you? What's her name—Faith? Hope? You know, the blonde." She took a quick breath and continued, "I matched the VIN number to a rental agency in Salt Lake. Your Jane Doe has a name. It's Judy Longacre." Doris paused a moment before adding, "She was so excited she couldn't wait to tell you. I'm surprised you don't know."

"Hope is the one in the hospital. There was an accident. She's unconscious—but last night, she kept trying to say a name. I'm pretty sure she said Judy—so maybe she was trying to tell me."

He finished his conversation with Doris, and made one more visit to Hope's room before heading on up to the Critical Care area.

Nancy looked up and winked when she saw Calder step off the elevator. "I thought you and Hope were roughing it out in the middle of the mountains. What brings you in town so early?"

"Too much to explain right now," Calder replied. "I understand Jane Doe has a name. Any change?"

"Ever so slight. There is minimal change in heart rate within a few minutes of someone speaking her name. But we aren't sure if it is her name, or the tone of voice she is responding to. It doesn't seem like much, but trust me, it's a huge step for a patient in a coma." Nancy always offered her medical update in layman's terms, making it easier to communicate with family members.

"Hope really made the most progress with her. I didn't want to get her expectations up, but when she was in here calling Judy by name, I noticed a change. It's as though she recognized her voice." She fingered her glasses and then removed them to get a close look at Calder. "You don't look so good yourself—is anything wrong?"

"When you get a break you need to go downstairs. Something happened to Hope. When I found her she was unconscious."

"Oh no. I'm so sorry. She's such a great girl—really has the touch. But I'm sure you know that," she said, reaching across the counter she squeezed Calder's hand. "I'll check on her—and make sure she gets on the best care," Nancy said, trying to reassure the tall cowboy cop.

"Nancy, please, if there are any changes to either Jane . . . ah . . . Judy, *or* Hope, call the station and Doris can reach me on the radio. Any change—Please—Call!" Calder left an emphatic request, before heading back down to check on Hope one last time before driving out to the ranch.

She looked so small and helpless lying there, blankets tucked around her, IV's connected to hands and arms. It was quiet and sterile in the room, everything in its place. In his mind he pictured her the way he had left her in the cabin, lying on the pallet in front of the soft glowing fire. Hair disheveled, lips full, swollen from a night of passion. He wished he could be her Prince Charming, and just place the awakening kiss on her lips. But it wasn't that easy. Nothing was that easy.

He picked up her hand and held it to his chest. "Hope, it's me Calder. I have to leave for a while. I'm going back to your cabin to find phone numbers for your family. I'll be back. Nancy will be in to check on you." He closed his eyes, a lump developed in his throat every time the thought of her not recovering entered his mind. He had to shake it. She was going to be fine, she had to be; somewhere in the night he realized he had fallen in love with her.

The drive back to the ranch took no time. Dust rumbled up behind the truck as he sped down the dirt road, past the saloon and slammed to a stop in front of the office. A cloud of dust proceeded Calder through the screen door.

"Hey! Slow down cowboy." Sarah asked, coming in from the back room. "How's Hope? Has she regained consciousness?"

"Not yet. The docs did a bunch of lab and x-rays; they should have the results soon. But . . ." The look of concern was written all over his face. Sarah put her arm around him and gave him a hug. "Come on—let me get you a cup of coffee, and something to eat. You look like you've had a rough night."

"Coffee I'll take. The food will have to wait. I'm looking for an emergency contact for Hope, did she happen to put one on her reservation?"

"Let me check." Sarah said, pulling the metal file drawer open to check her records. She pulled out a file and began flipping through forms.

"Roberts, Preston, Turner," she read the names off as she flipped through the pile. She hadn't gotten around to alphabetizing them. "Hayward, Longacre, here it is, Hanson. Hope Hanson."

"Wait a minute. Before Hanson. What did you say?" Calder was in shock. He really did need to get some sleep. That was the third time today he heard that name. It couldn't be a coincidence.

"Longacre. Roger and Joe Longacre, from Atlanta." She looked up at Calder; the look on his face said it all. "What? Calder tell me. That's the attorney and his little boy. What do they have to do with anything?"

"I'm not sure yet Sarah—but I could kiss you! You may have just solved the Jane Doe case." He took the registration forms for both Hope and the Longacre family and left the office. The screen door slammed shut behind him—then reopened and once again he stood by Sarah.

"What about Angela—do you have a registration on her?"

Sarah flipped through the forms, stopping at Lee. Angela Lee from Atlanta. Calder looked it over and put it with the others.

"Radio Doris as soon as the guests get back from the overnight. And don't let anyone leave the ranch until I get back," he commanded. A quick hug and Calder was once again back in his truck and on the road. Back to town.

CHAPTER 18

THE PRINTER RATTLED back and forth across the paper as it captured the information from the computer screen. Calder paced between the printer stand and desk; Doris rolled her eyes at him.

"You huffing and puffing isn't going to make it print any faster." Doris nagged. She loved to nag him about being impatient with electronics. He had all the patience in the world with animals and people, but when it came to machinery—too often it revealed a hidden temper. She had personally witnessed a microwave and TV meet an early demise due to Calder's impatient streak. Fearing her printer was next, she stood close, protecting it like a mother bear.

"Here you go Chief," she said, stapling the sheets together and handing them over to him.

He scanned the pages, then grabbed his revolver and hat and headed for the door.

"Bison One this is General Hospital," the old radio crackled with Nancy's voice. Calder stopped and turned, tired eyes fixed on the radio.

"This is Bison One. Go ahead General Hospital," Doris said in her most official sounding voice. She watched the muscle in Calder's cheek flex in anticipation.

"Tell the Chief his friend has had a setback. He should come right away."

"10-4," Doris replied, this time her voice cracked. Calder was out the door crossing the parking lot before she signed off.

*

Calder bolted from the elevator door and jogged down the hall to Hope's room. It was quiet; the bed was stripped of linen. The lump in his throat got thicker as he ran toward the nursing station. He didn't want to ask that question—fear ate at his gut. His head ached.

"Hope Hanson. Where is she?" he asked the first nurse he saw.

"Who are you looking for?"

"Hope Hanson. Room 234. Where is she?"

"Why don't you have a seat over there while I check," the nurse replied, trying to calm him down.

"I'm not sitting anywhere," he said, pushing past her, looking through the records hanging at the nurses' station.

"Please. You can't go back there," the nurse raised her voice, chasing after him. "Let me find out where your patient is. Calm down. Please."

He responded to her commanding voice—and when he looked up at her he realized his actions must have frightened her. But he didn't have time to worry about frightening her. He needed to know what happened to Hope.

"She's been transferred to ICU. Third floor." She barely got ICU out before Calder was at the elevator, frantically punching the button.

The third floor was a flurry of people and machines. Nancy spotted Calder coming toward the room and quickly intercepted him.

"She's going to be OK Calder. They're getting her stabilized now. She started convulsing when they intubated her. But they finally got her pumped and stabilized. And thank God. Her toxicology report showed an abnormally high amount of naratriptan in her system. She could have died."

He strained to look into the room. She was lying there, calm now, as doctors and nurses got her hooked up to monitors. Convulsions? Stomach pumped? "What the heck is naratriptan?" he asked, removing his hat and running his calloused hand through his dark hair.

"It's migraine medicine. Do you know if Hope suffered from migraines?" Nancy inquired. She walked him over to the family area and away from the action around Hope's room. She knew that he could see her soon, but for now, he needed to calm down.

"I don't know. She never mentioned anything about a headache." Calder was visibly shaken. He kept a close watch on the activity in her room. As long as it was slow and methodical, he knew she was all right.

"The x-rays and all other lab work came back normal. Then one report showed the possibility of a drug overdose. When they started to pump her stomach she aspirated and began convulsing. It was close, but they pulled her through it. They're running more labs; the next report should be closer to normal. It will work through her system, but then she should come out of it. The medicine is more than likely the reason she is unconscious."

Nancy sighed and took a deep breath. She hated to see drug overdoses, they could be so debilitating. In the back of her mind she knew there was always the possibility of brain damage. But she would let the doctor decide if he would disclose that.

A young doctor in scrubs knocked on the door of the lounge. "Nancy—the patient is stabilized. Keep an eye on her for us. Let me know when she regains consciousness."

"Can I see her now?" Calder asked, his face tense with concern.

"For a few minutes. Yes." Nancy replied. "And then you need to get some rest."

He entered the room slowly, quietly, so as not to disturb her. Pale hands lay exposed on top of the sheet—IV's feeding into veins. The memory of his mother, and the months she spent in the hospital came back to him in waves, assaulting his senses. As he stood there, it was as though he was standing in his mother's room—watching her breathe—waiting for her breath to stop. Waiting for her suffering to end.

He shook his head—he was tired and getting delirious. He couldn't think like that. This was Hope, not his mother. His mother had cancer that had spread to every vital organ she had. But Hope, Hope wasn't going to die—Hope had to live. And he couldn't allow himself to even think thoughts of death while he stood in her room.

He bent down and kissed her forehead. "Rest now. You had a rough day. I'll be back soon." His hand cupped her face as he softly kissed her cheek one more time before leaving.

*

Roger and Joe were sitting on the porch playing checkers when Calder pulled up in front of their cabin. Joe's freckles popped out even more from the sun he had gotten on the ride. When he recognized Calder's truck, he jumped up and ran over to greet the tall cowboy.

"How's Hope?" he asked, tugging on Calder's shirtsleeve. "Is she in the hospital?"

"She is, and the doctor says she is going to be just fine," Calder said, keeping an optimistic tone in his voice, not only for Joe, but for himself as well.

"Has she come to yet? Did she say what happened?" Roger asked, getting up from the pine bench and crossing the porch, to lean on the railing.

"Not yet, but she should soon." Calder replied. His face showed signs of exhaustion, but he remained upbeat. "Can we talk in private Roger?" he asked, not wanting to upset Joe any more than he was.

"Joe, you go inside now. I need to talk to Calder, alone. OK? We'll finish our game later, tiger," Roger said, winking at his young son.

The two men walked around the back of the truck and leaned against the tailgate. From an outsider's view they could have been friends for years, or neighbors getting together to talk about the weather. But they weren't, and Calder had to come clean.

"Roger, I don't know if you know this or not but I'm the Chief of Police in Buffalo." Calder gave him a few minutes to grasp that idea before continuing. "I've been working under-cover on a hit and run case. It happened right down the road from here, on Ranch property. I have reason to believe it was attempted murder."

"OK, but what does that have to do with me?" He looked puzzled, but wanted to know more.

"Your last name is Longacre?"

"Yes."

"Do you happen to know a Judy Longacre?" Calder finally asked. He was on track and he knew it. Adrenaline pumped through him—he was so close to solving the case.

"Judy is my wife," Roger said, "why, is something wrong?"

"I have reason to believe that the hit and run I mentioned is your wife. We tracked down the VIN number from the rental car; it was leased to a Judy Longacre of Atlanta. The local police have been trying to contact family in Atlanta, but have been unable so far. That's because you're here."

Roger looked as though he had been punched in the stomach. His face turned white. "What about Judy?" he demanded. "Where is she?"

"She's alive Roger, but she's been in a coma since last Saturday. It was a very bad accident. The car was totaled. Had it not been for Justin and Hope happening by, she may not have made it." Calder was careful not to provide too much information at once. He knew that Roger was experiencing a combination of guilt, responsibility, and grave concern. He had to give him time to absorb it all.

"I can't be certain that our Jane Doe is your wife until someone makes a positive ID."

"I'm on my way—but I can't take Joe. Not yet."

"Sarah will be more than happy to help. I'll let her know." Calder knew he had just dumped a lot of bad news on the man at one time, but also knew that now was the time he would get the most honest answers, at least about Angela. "One other question, Roger, about Angela. Do you know if she ever met Judy?"

"You don't think Angela had anything to do with this, do you?" He began rubbing his forehead and temples. "I was afraid she'd do something crazy, she was always talking about how she couldn't exist without me. She did attempt suicide once—but I never thought she'd go after Judy."

"So as far as you know, she didn't know Judy?"

"I don't know—she may have seen pictures. She's been to my house—during the time Judy left—and there are pictures of the family all around the den."

"Thanks. I know this is difficult on you, and I appreciate your honesty."

"There's something else you should probably know," Roger added, rubbing his hand across his mouth. "Angela's dad left her mother when she was about eleven. According to Angela it was blonde hair and red lips that lured him away. She hates blondes." He shook his head in disbelief. "I swear to God I never thought she would do anything like this. Never."

The men shook hands and Calder jumped back in his truck. Dust poured from under the tires as he shifted in reverse, then headed down the ranch road toward Angela's cabin.

The blinds were drawn and no one answered his knock. "Angela? Angela Lee?" He called out her name as his hand pounded against the door. "It's the Police, Angela. Open the door Angela," still no answer.

Jake came bounding up the steps at the sound of Calder's voice. He was wet from chasing geese and who knows what else in the pond, and excited to once again see Calder.

"Good boy. You stay here while I go get the master key from the office. Stay Jake—Guard!" his voice commanded the big black lab. Jake barked; his tail wagged as he looked from the door to Calder and back to the door.

"Guard," Calder repeated, and then ran toward the office. He was almost to the door when he heard the barks. It was Jake, in his loud, agitated bark. It was a bark that Calder was familiar with—it conveyed a sense of urgency. He turned and ran back to the cabin.

The door was open. Jake stood at the entrance, the fur on his neck raised, his barking continuous.

"Get him out of here" she screamed from somewhere inside the cabin.

"Police," Calder said, flashing a badge as he stepped around Jake at the cabin entrance.

She stood inside, with a broom raised above her head. "Get him out of my way or I'll kill him," she screamed, waving the broom frantically.

"I'd put that broom down if I were you," Calder said calmly, then turned his attention to Jake. "OK Jake. Good boy. Sit. Stay." The dog quieted down, but kept his eyes fixed on Angela.

"What the hell do you think you're doing, breaking in to my cabin?" She was agitated and still screaming. "I'll have you arrested for this!"

"Fine. But first—I have a warrant here, to search your cabin." He shoved the document at her, tired of her shrill voice. "And unless you want that dog all over you, I'd advise you to sit down and shut up."

"But . . . you have no right!" she continued to protest.

"I have every right," he said and began searching the living room and kitchen for personal items. He checked the refrigerator and rummaged through books and magazines. In the bathroom, he looked through bags of makeup and creams. Opening the medicine cabinet he hit pay dirt. Prescriptions—made out to Angela Lee. *Amerge. Take only as directed.* Labels warning of drowsiness and not to operate machinery covered the side of the bottle. He placed it in a baggie along with other prescriptions and walked back into the living room.

"That's mine. Those are legal prescriptions."

"I'll have to verify that Angela, and just what are these prescriptions for?"

"Migraines. I get terrible migraines and if you don't give them back to me I'll sue you and your backwoods police department." She puffed nervously on a cigarette, it's tip smeared with her red lipstick.

Watching her, it clicked. "Don't you know that's bad for your health?" Calder commented casually. He scanned the cabin and found another ashtray—filled with red-rimmed cigarette butts. He walked across the room and emptied the ashtray into another baggie.

Her face paled.

"You're under arrest Angela Lee, for the attempted murder of Hope Hanson." He read her rights, handcuffed her, and escorted her outside and into the backseat of his truck. Jake followed along and took his place in his crate, this time facing the cab—keeping a watchful eye on the defiant captive in the back of the truck.

CHAPTER 19

HE SAT IN a chair nearby and watched. The late afternoon sun lulled her to sleep. She sat on a chaise, propped up with pillows and a cotton throw covering her legs. A bouquet of fresh flowers from Susan and John, along with a note scribbled in Susan's left hand, was perched on the table next to her. A book lay folded on her chest, rising and falling with the rhythm of each breath. Strands of golden hair escaped from the large brimmed hat, and fluttered in the breeze around her face. And now, as the sunset faded and the sky turned shades of pink and blue, he covered her with a blanket.

She was out of danger now, and would soon be going home. Home—back to Charlotte, a city without mountains. Back to her real life. Back to a life he would never fit in to.

Somewhere between the time she first laughed at him on the plane and now, his life had changed. Drastically. He had been physically attracted to her from the moment he set eyes on her; but he never thought a little flirtation could go this far, this fast. When had it happened? On the mesa? When he watched her with Judy? Or the night he watched her by the corral? There was so much about this woman that he loved, yet there was so much about her that he didn't know. He had to find out before she left, he had to know if she felt the same. But then what—what if she did? It wouldn't be right to ask her to move across country—from North Carolina to Wyoming. Far from family, friends, and the life she had chosen. No. He couldn't do that. It wouldn't be fair.

His mother had sacrificed everything to move to the hills of Wyoming to be with his father. They had met during the war, in San Francisco before they were shipped off to Nam. His mother was an army nurse, his dad—infantry. They fell in love amidst the tragedy of war—sharing the nightmares of reality. And when they returned, she followed him back to Wyoming, giving up all she had known and loved to be with him. His mother sacrificed everything she loved, for love. And as much as he knew her heart was in Wyoming, her soul longed for California, for home. She finally got to go back, just before she became ill. Calder took both his mom and dad to a family reunion in California. She laughed and sparkled with conversation of old friends and family, and glowed with the moonlight as they strolled along San Francisco Bay. She said that trip meant the world to her—and he knew it did.

No. He would never ask Hope to move. Not for love or money—it wasn't fair.

The night breeze rustled through the trees. Hope stirred, opening her eyes and smiling at the cowboy sitting next to her.

"Hey. Why didn't you wake me?" she asked, sitting up in the chaise. She lifted the blanket and patted her hand on the empty space next to her on the chaise. "Come here, and sit with me. Keep me warm."

"Are you sure," he asked, concerned about the three cracked ribs she had.

"Sure. You know the old saying, no pain, no gain," she lifted the blanket again. The light from the outside lanterns flickered in the breeze, revealing long shapely legs under the blanket.

Calder lowered himself onto the chaise, careful not make any quick movement for fear of causing her pain.

"How's Judy doing, did you see her today?" Hope asked, knowing her Jane Doe had a long recovery ahead of her.

"Good, real good. She still has a long rehab in front of her but I ran into Roger in town and he said that he rented a house nearby the hospital, so he and Joe can stay close until she's up for the flight back to Atlanta. He's so happy she's regained consciousness and is on the road to recovery."

"It's a miracle. The way she looked that night, like a pretzel folded around the steering wheel. Thank God for that airbag—that is the only thing that saved her."

"That and the fact that you and Justin came along just at the right time. It was your quick action that saved her, and we all know that." He beamed with pride as he spoke. Had it not been for her training, concern, and persistence with the case—he wasn't sure if he ever would have solved it. Well he probably would have once Roger and Joe returned to Atlanta, but by then all the clues would have disappeared—it would have been all circumstantial evidence tying Angela to the accident. Judy didn't remember who ran her off the road. If it wasn't for the red lipstick on the cigarette butts—the one he picked up at the accident site was a match to those in Angela's cabin. And after that—she confessed to everything, attacking

Hope with the shovel, ransacking her cabin, and even lacing her water with her migraine medicine. She was really messed up.

As if reading his mind, Hope asked, " And what about Angela?"

Calder shook his head in wonder. "You amaze me Hope. That woman tried to kill you and you're still worried about her."

"She's messed up Calder. I feel sorry for her. But don't get me wrong—I'm glad she's behind bars where she belongs. She was crying out for help—look at all her attempted suicides." She drew in a breath and rested her head on Calder's shoulder. There was something about being near him that made her soul rest easy. "Just think of the damage she could have done to little Joe. That's what worries me most."

The stars began to appear one by one in the night sky. At first, they appeared as a vague dot in the twilight. But as darkness claimed the night, they lit up the sky like sparklers on the fourth of July. They sat for a while, enjoying the evening and each other's company without speaking. There was so much to say; so much she wanted to tell him. But why? The case was solved and she would go home soon. He hadn't mentioned anything about continuing their relationship. And on second thought, did they even have a relationship? Lying next to him on the chaise she wished they did.

"Count a hundred stars," Hope whispered. Her hand reached for Calder's under the blanket.

"Count a hundred stars, and your dream will come true," he replied. "That is if you believe in legends and fairy tales." The scar on his cheek jumped with the tightening of his jaw, a reflex that Hope had become attuned to.

"Bah Humbug yourself!" She replied to his change in attitude. "Just because I have a couple of cracked ribs doesn't mean . . ."

"No Hope. I was thinking about us. What now? You said so yourself. This isn't going to lead anywhere. As soon as you're well enough to get back on a plane you'll be gone. Gone from Snowy Creek, gone from Wyoming, and gone from me. So why make things more complicated?"

"So what are you saying—all this between us *was* just for looks—for a cover?" She could feel the heat rising in her face. Pain shot through her ribcage as she took in a deep breath.

"Well, there's no need for you to pretend anymore," Calder suggested, giving her an out yet praying she wouldn't take it.

"What you're saying is now that I'm sick the fun's over?" Hope was livid. She drug her legs over the chaise and tried to roll off and up using the pillows around her. She gasped in pain, trying to hide it from him.

"Hey—wait a minute. What are you trying to do, kill yourself?" Calder jumped up to assist her. "If you wanted to get up you should have told me! I'm here to help you."

"Well not any more. I can get around on my own now, and I'll be leaving soon. I'm sure you've got plenty of other things to do than play nursemaid to me."

"Hope—listen to me. Listen to you. You are the one that said you didn't come to Wyoming for a cowboy—you came here to relax, for vacation. Look what I've put you through." Even though he felt responsible for her condition, he thanked God for every minute he had spent with her.

"Yeah. Thanks . . . for nothing," she added, in spite of what she felt in her heart. She wanted him to ask her to stay; she wanted him to say he had fallen in love with her. But instead she was hearing the old let's be friends way to end a relationship. She couldn't bear it. "I think it's time to say goodbye Calder. You should go."

He stood up and glared at her. The muscle in his jaw twitched several times before he spoke. "C'mon Jake. We don't stay where we're not wanted." Jake rose from his spot in the corner and diligently followed Calder down the steps, disappearing into the night.

She heard the deep rumble of the truck's diesel engine and gritty squeal of the tires against dirt as he drove away. Tears welled in her eyes and pain shot through her chest. This time she wasn't sure if it was her ribs or her heart breaking.

She lay back down on the chaise and between sobs, began counting stars.

*

Calder cursed all the way home. He cursed himself, love, Wyoming . . . everything but Hope. Why was she acting like that? Wasn't she the one who kept reminding him that there was no relationship? So why did she get so upset when he gave her an out? The night he spent with her had changed everything for him, but obviously not for her. The days following while she lay unconscious in the hospital, he realized how important she was to him. Those long nights spent by her side, holding her hand and telling her all about his hopes and dreams, had made him understand how important love is—it's the only thing. Love is the tie that binds, that entwines two hearts. He had felt it from the moment he met her—there was something special between them. He felt it with her that night in her cabin. And he knew she did too. But he couldn't just ask her to give up her life to remain in Wyoming with him. He wouldn't. And from the way she'd been acting since the accident—it was as though she couldn't wait to get on that plane and leave. She mentioned it every time they were together—and he didn't need any more reminders. The clock was ticking way too fast to please him.

Pulling into the drive that ended at his log cabin, Calder resigned to throw himself into work, and busy himself with chores around the cabin. He had wanted to finish that extra addition for his dad, and it looked like now would be the time to get it done. Anything to keep his mind off Hope Hanson—and the fact that in a few days she would be flying out of his life for good.

Crap. Why did life have to be so damn complicated? He reached down and patted the top of Jake's head as he opened his front door. The phone rang as he walked in; he picked it up on the second ring.

"Calder Elliott?" an unfamiliar voice asked.

"Speaking."

"This is Cliff Hanson, Hope's brother, returning your call."

*

Sarah Porter had made it her business to begin each day bringing a tray of breakfast and hot pot of coffee to Hope's cabin since her accident. She talked of events around the ranch, how the children loved the rooster roundup and pig wrestling. And as new guests arrived, talk of the events that led to Hope's accident and Angela's arrest subsided. Sarah and Sam both agreed that publicity was good to a point—but the arrest was a bit more publicity than they wanted. Snowy Creek returned to normal. Horses, hiking, and good food were the main subject of conversation. But today, she hoped the conversation would be different. Today she brought along a bouquet of yellow roses.

Hope struggled to get off the sofa when she saw Sarah coming up the steps to the cabin. The severe pain in her chest was still there—but each day movement became easier. It would soon be time for her to leave Snowy Creek, and she wasn't sure she was ready. It had been a week since Calder had stormed off her porch with Jake. A week with no word—nothing. Perhaps she had been right—the case was solved and since she was in no condition for any wild lust-filled nights, he had no reason to see her. Maybe this was the best way.

"Good morning! Isn't this a great morning?" Sarah asked, setting the tray down on the kitchen table. She took the roses off the tray and placed them in the center of the table, carefully separating each stem and taking time to smell each individual bud. Fussing over them as Hope had never seen her fuss. She seemed happier than usual this morning and Hope was anxious to find out what was going on. By now, she knew Sarah well enough to know that she was dying to tell her something.

"OK. What gives?" Hope asked, finally taking the bait.

"Well for one thing—aren't these the prettiest yellow roses?" Sarah glanced sideways at Hope, looking just like the cat that just ate the canary. "Wouldn't you like to read the card?"

Hope's eyes widened. Dare she hope they were from Calder? The local florist had been kept busy with flowers from her office, Susan and John, her mother and her brother Cliff. On the last trip, the florist told her he hadn't had that much business at Snowy Creek since Sam and Sarah got married! But with each delivery, Hope's dreams were dashed. As nice as it was for family and friends to remember her, she secretly wished one of the deliveries had been from Calder.

The card was hidden among leaves and baby's breath. It truly was a beautiful arrangement—short, full-bodied yellow roses, tucked neatly into a blue and white container, laced with baby's breath and fern, were all compacted into an elegant arrangement. It was not the long stemmed type arrangement that Hope was accustomed to seeing. Another reason not to believe they were from Calder. But then again . . . she opened the card and right away noticed his structured printing. Staring at the words, it took her a moment to read the message. *The blue in the vase reminds me of your eyes, the yellow roses—your hair. But not even the beauty of the roses can compare to the beauty I see in you. I'll never forget you. Love Calder*

"So what does this mean?" she asked, turning toward Sarah who obviously thought she'd be thrilled with the flowers. "I'll never forget you? Is that instead of goodbye and good luck?" Hope's temper flared. It was obvious from the message that Calder wanted her to leave, wanted her to get as far away from Wyoming as possible, and the sooner the better.

"No. Don't you see? He signed it Love Calder." Sarah tried to intervene. "Hope, I believe he's in love with you and afraid you don't feel the same for him. He's trying to save face."

"Well," she replied in a huff, "if he really loved me he'd bring himself over here and tell me, instead of sending flowers and a . . . a half hearted message. Sarah—you and Sam and everyone here has become like family to me. You have no idea how grateful I am for all you've done. But if Calder thinks for one minute that roses and a scribbled note are all I want—then he's not the man I thought he was." Hope took in a deep breath and winced in pain. "After all we've been through these past weeks, I can't believe he'd let me leave without saying goodbye."

She threw the note on the table and trudged outside. The brisk morning air was what she needed to calm down and cool off. She shouldn't have gotten upset with Sarah—she was only the messenger. But, she wondered, had Calder sent these via the florist or brought them himself? The card was sealed, so it had to be the latter; and if that was the case, why didn't he bring them to her personally? Love her?—at this point Hope swore he must be counting the minutes until she was gone.

"Hope, listen to me. I don't know what happened between you and Calder and maybe it's none of my business. But I have to tell you that not a day has gone by that he hasn't called in to check on you. And not a day goes by that Sam hasn't asked where he's been. I've never seen him act like this before. When we ask him where he's been he always has the same pat reply. 'Busy'." She shook her head and pursed her mouth before speaking again. "I'd be more than happy to tell him you loved the flowers and hoped to see him before you leave . . ." Sarah tried her best to persuade Hope to offer an olive branch.

"Don't you dare! Sarah, really! I've been thinking about things and well . . . maybe it's best this way. Yes I care about him but we hardly know each other. What would we do—have a long distance relationship? We both know that wouldn't work."

"Sam proposed to me on our second date," Sarah replied grinning from ear to ear.

"Well that just proves how right the two of you are together. You *both* knew you were in love." Hope sighed and picked up the note. She ran her finger across the writing.

"Thanks Sarah. And thank Calder for the beautiful roses. But really, honestly, I think it's better this way."

CHAPTER 20

JUSTIN EMERGED FROM Hope's cabin carrying her briefcase, and closed the door behind him. He had already loaded her other bags in the back of the Snowy Creek truck. It was just the two of them. She was going back before the weekend rush—knowing the airports wouldn't be as hectic, and hoping to avoid too many sentimental goodbyes. Most of the wranglers were working today—it was a day like most others during the end of the season at Snowy Creek. Wide-eyed youngsters marveled at the horses and mountains—and dreamed of riding the range with the likes of the Lone Ranger, or Butch Cassidy and the Sundance Kid.

Hope turned around for one last look from her cabin. The natural beauty that surrounded her was breathtaking. That would soon change. Drastically. The noise of traffic and crush of people involved in city life would soon slap her in the face. Even though her hometown was small compared to many cities, she would never be able to step outside and breathe in fresh mountain air, and witness the awesome beauty that was around every corner in Wyoming. No. Once she returned it would be heat and humidity. And a life she wanted to forget. She couldn't believe that the past three and a half weeks had such a profound impact on her life. She feared returning home, returning to the life she had chosen after Brian died. Because now she knew what she needed to do, what she wanted to do. After recuperating at home under her mother's care, she was going to start looking for a job in nursing. That was where her heart was—it wasn't in the fast life she had been living over the past five years. It was in caring and giving. She had felt alive again these past weeks, alive as the real Hope Hanson.

Sarah and Sam were waiting by the truck.

"Here's a little something for you to remember us by," Sarah said, handing Hope a package wrapped in red bandana cloth. "No need to open it now, I just hope you can find a spot for it in your bag."

"You've been so kind to me. Thank you. For everything." Tears welled in her eyes as she hugged Sarah and Sam. "I'll never forget my visit to Snowy Creek."

"And you know you are more than welcome to return. Any time. You just let us know and we'll get your cabin ready—on us" Sam added in his normally gruff voice. His eyes twinkled as he spoke. "Hopefully the next time will be all rest and relaxation."

They said their goodbyes and Hope got situated in the truck. Her ribs were getting better every day, but she still needed the aid of a pillow for support. She arranged it around her as they pulled away and headed out through the canopy of pines away from the ranch.

They rode quietly down the winding mountain road, slowing down slightly as they reached the turn of the accident. It was hard to believe that only a few weeks had passed since that night when they happened upon the wreck. Her mind raced with vivid memories of that night, Judy's bloodied face, and Calder's strong arms folding around her, once again offering a soft place to fall.

"Since I have a couple of hours before my flight, do you have time to run me by the hospital? I'd like to check on Judy before I leave."

"Yes ma'am. No problem." Justin replied. "I'm sure she would be glad to see you too." His blonde hair poked out from under the brim of his hat. "I could stop by the police station too if you'd like?" he added. He tried to sound nonchalant but his grin gave him away.

She shot him a disapproving glance. "No Justin. I don't think so. And I believe you are wearing enough hats at Snowy Creek without adding that of matchmaker." Hope appreciated his attempt, but the one who really needed to make an attempt was either too busy, too stubborn, or just didn't want to.

"Just thought I'd offer." He added with a wink.

They talked about the rodeo and living in Charlotte, and before long he pulled the Snowy Creek truck up to the hospital entrance and carefully helped Hope climb down.

"Do you want me to get you a wheelchair?" he asked, enjoying his role of protector.

"No thanks. I can walk. I don't want anyone to get the idea I'm checking in. Been there; done that!" She shot him a teasing smile, "I won't be too long."

Nancy was behind the desk updating a patient chart when the elevator door opened.

"Well hey—how's my favorite patient?" she asked, taking off her glasses and smiling widely at Hope.

"Getting better every day. Don't they ever give you a day off around here?" Hope asked, knowing how staff appreciated having their long hours acknowledged.

"I'm a glutton for punishment. One of the other nurses needed the day for her daughter's birthday; so I thought I'd help out. And I'm glad I did, I got to see you." Nancy placed her hand on Hope's back and rubbed gently. "How are those ribs?"

"Well as you can see, I'm still using my pillow for protection," she said, rearranging it under her arm.

"I've been thinking," Nancy added, suddenly serious. "I know you've been talking of returning to nursing. And before you got away I wanted to run something by you. We're hiring, and I know from experience you are exactly what we are looking for. So before we let a great nurse walk out the door, I wanted to offer you a job." She rested her glasses on the end of her nose and ruffled through papers on her desk. "Here. Here's an application. Please tell me you'll think about it. You'd be a perfect fit here in Buffalo."

"Thanks Nancy. I take that as a compliment." She looked down at the application and studied it for a few minutes. "This is rather tempting. But before I make any decisions, I've got to get back home and sort things out."

"Well, I thought I'd try. I know it's got to be difficult to think about uprooting and moving away from your home. But I thought, just in case they aren't hiring down there, and you really wanted to get back into it . . ."

As Nancy rambled on about all the benefits of working at Buffalo General, Hope realized just how easy it *would* be for her to leave Charlotte. She had no family there. She was renting an apartment that she wasn't crazy about, and as far as her friends, well, they hadn't even missed her until she called the office requesting additional time off because of the broken ribs. And all her boss had to offer was some tacky comment about her not being Annie Oakley and she shouldn't have gone out there in the first place. Not a lot of sympathy. Friends? No. In reality they were more like drinking buddies, acquaintances that passed through her life. Nice people, but far from life long friends.

Hope walked across the ward into Judy's room wondering what her life would be like now if Judy hadn't been run off the road that night. It was strange how life's twists and turns can suddenly bring everything into perspective.

Judy was resting and Hope decided not to waken her. She sat down in the chair next to the bed, knowing the peace that comes from sitting with someone for comfort. The swelling was mostly gone, but Judy's face still carried the greenish yellow marks of severe bruising. And considering all the internal damage and broken bones, she still had a lengthy hospital stay and even longer rehab. But she was alive. And she was expected to return to a full, normal lifestyle. Hope sat with her for about ten minutes before a man appeared at the door. She smiled at him, slowly eased out of her chair, and crossed the room to join Roger in the hall.

"She's resting," Hope said, affirming what Roger had noticed as he looked in the room.

"And how are you doing?" he asked. He had spoken to Hope at length before he and Joe had checked out of the ranch, and apologized for all the pain and suffering he had caused. He felt responsible for everything; his philandering ways had caused a lot of distress.

"Better. I'm flying out today. Heading home. I just wanted to stop in one more time to check on her before I left. But I didn't want to wake her. Please give her my best and let her know that I'll be thinking of her, and know that she will have a full and speedy recovery. Mostly because of you and Joe. She has every reason in the world to get better. Love." Hope reached up and kissed Roger on the cheek. "And give little Joe a hug for me. Tell him I would have delivered it myself but I'm still having a bit of a problem getting around. The ribs, you know."

"I can't thank you enough Hope. You and Justin saved Judy's life. Joe and I can't begin to express what we feel."

"Oh, but you have. In a strange way—Judy saved me as much as I saved her." She smiled a reflective smile.

He looked at her questioningly.

"Maybe I can explain it to you someday. Bye Roger; take care." She took one more look around the ward and watched Roger take her place by Judy's side, patiently waiting to once again be a family. To once again take his place by her side. Guilt was often life's toughest instructor.

Hope gathered her pillow to her side and leaned against the back of the elevator as it slowly slipped between floors. She was on her way back to a life she no longer cared about. Just what was her future going to bring? Just as Angela was responsible for Judy's wreck and her broken ribs, she alone was responsible for her future, and she alone held the key to happiness, to a life of fulfillment and love.

As the elevator doors opened, she knew she had one more stop to make before she boarded the plane.

CHAPTER 21

THE SNOWY CREEK truck was nowhere in sight. Hope walked to the edge of the canopied breezeway to get a better view of the parking lot. Shielding her eyes with her hand, she scanned the lot for the white truck. It wasn't there—Justin probably decided to run an errand while waiting, so she carefully lowered herself onto the park bench in front of the hospital, waiting for him to return.

He watched her from a distance. Having positioned himself away from the door, out of her line of sight. The pain he witnessed on her face as she slowly settled onto the bench felt like a knife piercing his heart. He had to be kidding himself if he thought he could talk to her without showing how he cared. Not today. Not with Hope.

She was about to leave him—fly out of his life. His only saving grace was the fact that she would be back for Angela's trial. No telling when that would be. Angela's lawyer from Atlanta was trying everything to get a change of venue. But even though Judy, her family, and Angela were from Atlanta, the crime had occurred in Buffalo. And she was charged and to be tried under Wyoming law.

Hope was a key witness—thanks to Calder. His interest in her had gotten her involved over her head. He was responsible for her pain. Had he gone home that night instead of giving in to his passions for Hope, he would have known that Doris had put a name on their Jane Doe. He would have made the connection to Angela before that fateful ride. He was the detective—he should have been there. But no. He gave in to his passion, to her tender mouth, her soft skin, her welcoming arms and body. The passion that raced between them was so fiery, so erotic, nothing could have pulled him away from her. Yes. It was his fault she winced in pain. And while his pride kept him from telling her how he felt, hearing her say he must be crazy to think she could ever live in Wyoming—with a cowboy cop and his aging father, was his real fear. Yeah. He must be crazy.

A breeze came up from across the parking lot, ruffling tree leaves and delivering the scent of rain. It was in the distance, but the sky was beginning to gray and cloud up. Hope pulled her jacket closer to her. Errant wisps of golden blonde hair fluttered around her face, teasing his vision. What did he have to lose? He had to talk with her one last time.

He approached from behind and she turned slowly, as though she sensed him approaching. Her eyes were soft blue pools. There was no anger, no pain. Just concern, caring, and love.

"I knew you were there," she said, "I can feel it when you're near, it's like a feeling of warmth surrounds me; it's very comforting." She studied him, knowing this may be her last chance for any private conversation. For any intimacy—for if she didn't break through that barrier now, she never would. She would rebuild her wall, and weeks and months would only add to its impenetrable mortar. No—it was now or never. She had to be honest.

"I'd ask you how you are but I can see you're still in pain." Calder stood motionless, the muscle that ran through the scar in his cheek tightened; he swallowed and looked down at his boots, then back up to her welcoming eyes. "I'm nervous Hope. I feel like I'm sixteen again. I don't know what to say."

"Walk with me Calder," she said, slowly rising from the bench.

He reached out for her. His strong arms surrounded her as he helped her to her feet, and remained there as she relaxed into him. It felt good to rest her bruised muscles—to have him support her. She trusted him and felt safe in his arms.

"We don't have to walk if you don't feel up to it."

"It's the getting up and down that hurt's. I can walk fine." She reached out for his arm. They strolled down the sidewalk with no destination in mind.

"I'm on my way to the airport," Hope said, trying to instill a sense of urgency and importance to their conversation. This wasn't time for idle chatter. If he had anything to say, she wanted him to know that now was the time to say it.

"You won't be able to go back to work for awhile. Why the rush to leave?"

"My mom is coming up to help me while I recuperate. Nothing a little time and chicken soup can't heal," she said, chuckling, "my only fear there is that while I love my mom, three or four days are usually the max for a visit. This will be a test."

"You know, you'll need to come back for the trial. You're our key witness."

She stiffened. Her nerves rattled a bit—here she was trying to talk about them and all he wanted to talk about was the upcoming trial.

"I'll be here. You don't have to worry about that." Her chin automatically raised in defiance.

"What I'm worried about is how I'm going to make it here without you." He said it. He was finally being brutally honest—with himself.

She stopped abruptly and searched his face. She was afraid he was teasing her, but his eyes were dark and serious, and she held her breath waiting for him to speak.

"There's something I need to tell you Hope. And maybe, after I finish, you'll understand why I can't ask you to stay."

Her heart pounded violently in her chest, and the muscles supporting her ribs began to quiver in pain. But she stood there, braced for heartbreak. Now or never . . .

"You know that my mom died recently, and that my mom and dad were everything to each other. What you don't know, is that she was from San Francisco—and when they got married she had to leave everything she loved behind. And as happy as she was with her life here with me and my dad—she grieved for home. Her eyes would linger on every add depicting the California Coast, or the Golden Gate bridge. It's as though part of her never left—maybe she was like the song and really did leave her heart in San Francisco—at least part of it. What's sad is that to this day, I don't know if my dad was ever aware of her homesickness. But I was all too aware of it. And it's what I wanted to give her the most before she died." He swallowed hard to rid himself of the lump in his throat. His eyes glazed with emotion. Hope leaned into him, hugging him as best she could without wrapping her arms around him. They walked on and he continued. "I sent them on a vacation the year Mom died. Even though the cancer was eating her up, I've never seen her happier than in those pictures. It's as though she belonged. She had reconnected." He paused and turned to Hope. "I never want to put someone I love in that position. I can't ask you to stay."

"But," she hesitated, biting her bottom lip, "you can tell me if you want me to stay. Can't you?"

"Is there a difference?"

She sighed and looked away. Why was he making this so difficult? She took a long breath and decided to shoot for the moon. "I wish I could explain how total I feel when I'm with you. My senses are charged with you, all my emotions become heightened. Sexually—I'm raw with passion when you're near. But at the same time I feel an odd sense of comfort in your arms—a sense of being protected but not controlled. I trust you Calder, and as a rule I don't trust men." She bared her soul with that statement and knew it. But she did trust him, with all of her heart, with all of her being. Somewhere along the way, somewhere among the wind and trees and mountains, Calder Elliott had touched her soul with a gentleness and passion she could never let go.

He placed a finger to her lips.

She feared he was about to rip out her heart and make a mockery of her words. No. God. Please. Don't play games with me, she thought. The seconds between them weighed heavy on her heart.

Calder brushed the hair from her face and cupped her chin in his hand. He kissed her forehead, and cheek. Then gently lowered his mouth to hers. His kiss was hot. Inviting. Gentle. Forever.

"I want you to stay Hope. But . . ." his voice trailed off, "only if it's a change you would have made without me—only if the mountains and the trees, the rivers and streams have captured your soul. Because no matter what happens to me, they will always be there for you."

"And that is something I have to come to grips with. You're a cop—and there is always that chance something dreaded will happen and you won't come home." She shook her head reliving that night in Charlotte, and then continued. "I was engaged to a cop who was killed during a drug bust. It devastated me, sent me spiraling out of control. I found myself again. Here. I'm not sure if I can separate the whole experience. I believe the mountains and vistas will always take my breath away, just like you."

Hope glanced down at her watch. It was getting close to time to head to the airport; Calder realized it too.

"I know . . . the clock is ticking." Calder's voice was flat. "Hope, I want to marry you, but I don't want to scare you off. I know we haven't known each other that long, but if you stayed here, with me at my cabin, until your ribs healed? My dad would love the company, and it would give us some time to get to know each other without the pressure of a case."

"There will always be a case Calder. I know that. I'll always worry when you walk out the door." She smiled and ran her finger along the outline of his face. "It's part of my job."

"I want to learn all there is to know about you Hope, every detail, so I'll know why I love you so much."

She melted at the sound of those words. It was what she had hoped for, prayed for. She rested her head on his chest and breathed in his comforting sexy scent. She was in love with this man and wanted to tell the world. She was finally home.

Distant thunder rumbled, drawing their attention skyward. It was beginning to look treacherous. A late summer storm was rolling in from across the mountains.

"Weather like that would be tough on those ribs, bouncing around in a small plane," Calder quipped, suggesting she stay.

She relaxed in his arms and looked up at him. Her gaze flirted—her smile enticed. "Did you arrange for this weather?" she asked, glancing up toward the smoky gray sky.

"You caught me," Calder confessed. "Last night, I looked up to the heavens and prayed that the mountains had touched your spirit and that I had touched your heart - that you loved me, and would want to stay here with me. And then, one by one, I counted a hundred stars!"

The End